ISBN: 9780578789576

First Printing 2021

AnnaJWalner.com

SILVER DAWN PUBLISHING

GARKAIN

Book One of the Uluru Legacy

COMING HOME

Amelia stared at the man in the seat next to her, watching him breathe deeply in a dreamless sleep as they flew over the Pacific Ocean on their way back to the States.

She would be going home to tie up loose ends and delete her former life completely. Roan would be seeing the States for the first time, both of them making the most of their three months before returning to a life that would be a huge commitment for them.

A life that she never dreamed of, but now she couldn't imagine any other way. She still pondered the events of the last few weeks, and their future to come. How they would unite two separate worlds as one. How they would lead a new community into the future, reshaping it and bringing fresh ideas to an archaic society.

For now though, she tried to push the thoughts from her mind. This was their time together now. Their last three months of freedom.

Amelia brushed the hair from Roan's forehead as she watched him for a while. It was hard for her to completely process the events that led up to this moment. Only a few months ago she'd been a girl with no family. And now she was a daughter, a sister, a granddaughter, and in December, she'd be a wife.

Twenty-five years of wondering and questions. Imagining the why's, searching on the internet for a possible connection. Taking the DNA test two years ago and signing up for the online registry. Bouncing from foster home to home, never finding a place to fit. If she'd only known, if she only had a clue what awaited her . . .

The two weeks she spent with the Uluru Colony, or just the Colony, as they called it, had changed her in ways she never imagined were possible. Psychically, emotionally, and spiritually. She was, quite honestly, a completely different person.

The things she had seen and experienced defied explanation for anyone outside of their community. She had been Unbound, no longer tethered by human rules or laws. What she was now must remain a secret to anyone outside of their hidden world. No one could ever know. Not her friends or her family in the States. No one. It was safest that way.

So much had happened in such a short time. She'd met her family, and fallen in love with the country, was intrigued by the culture of her people, and made the decision to accept a proposition that would change everything. She had agreed to things she never thought she would. Become something she never thought existed. And found a life worth dying for.

Only three months, she thought sadly. She had such a short time to sever all ties with her former life, adopted family and friends, and return back home to her duty, and her future.

Something that she was looking forward to. They were her real family now. The Colony. Michelle, Robert, and Ambrose. Anatole and Phoebe, and of course Roan. This was the life that she had chosen, and the reason for her birth. The experiment of her adoption had been successful, and it was time for her to take up her position as a leader.

For now, she had to make the most of her time, putting in her notice at work, and selling the home she had worked so hard to buy. She'd decided to tell everyone that she had taken a job in Australia. She would tell them she needed a change of scenery. A fresh start. She would promise to keep in touch. The less they knew the better.

She'd fed just before getting on the plane, she made sure to see to that before the long flight. But she was starting to get hungry again, and peanuts wouldn't do it for her. She needed a mid flight snack, one that wasn't on the menu. With just over six hours left, one good meal should hold her until they landed.

She looked at Roan again, asleep next to her. She pressed the call button on her seat, as a friendly flight attendant came quickly to see what she needed. First class did indeed have its perks.

Amelia stared at her for a moment, then followed the attendant into the bathroom. Her mouth was already burning, her gums tearing as she tasted her own blood for a moment.

Closing the door to the spacious restroom, the attendant held out her arm. No words were exchanged, no fuss, and no drama. Amelia's double set of fangs emerged, as she punctured the cocoa colored skin, tasting the friendly attendant's blood.

She drank for several seconds, filling her mouth and her stomach, before she withdrew. The marks were so small, hardly noticeable, as she brushed her thumb over them. The natural coagulant in her saliva stopped the flow of blood, and the attendant went on her way casually, as if nothing strange at all had happened.

She took a quick look in the mirror, smiling and rinsing the red blood from between her teeth. Yes, she had changed during her time with the Colony. She was immortal, Unbound, and now engaged to a man she'd never met until last week, who sat sleeping peacefully on the plane next to her.

She made her way back to her seat, replaying the trip, the events, the surprises, and her death all over again. Roan was still asleep as she knew he would be.

She slipped into her seat, and put her earbuds back in, letting the gentle music drown out the emotions and the sounds around her.

MEETING MOM

Amelia Wilson had been found at the local hospital in Houston, TX when she was just a baby. Sitting outside the sliding glass doors with no note and no clue of who might have left her.

Two years ago, she took a chance and ordered the DNA kit, sending it in and waiting, scrolling through distant matches until an alert popped up on her phone one day:

Phoebe Alura. Listed as Close Family, Biological Mother. Location: Perth, Australia.

She frantically opened the app and paused on the empty message. There were so many things she wanted to ask, to say. So many things she'd imagined for so many years. And now she was drawing a blank.

She was still deep in thought as another alert sounded on her phone, showing up on the screen. A message sent. Just now. She stared at the phone, looking at the waiting message as the tip of her finger hovered just above the icon. She pressed it, watching the short message appear on her phone.

"We've been searching for you." It said.

A shiver ran down Amelia's spine as she read and re-read the short message. Thinking of how to respond. So many questions sprang from one sentence.

Who were 'we', and why were *they* looking for her?

She started a message, then erased it. Then started it again. How do you even begin to answer a message like that? She thought.

She decided to be direct, typing her message and pressing send: We should talk. Call me. (936) 638-4214.

She had no idea what time it was in Australia, but whatever time it was, Phoebe was apparently awake.

A few minutes later her phone rang, a string of numbers showed on the screen, with the location under it stating simply: Australia.

She ran through all the possible things that she could say as she watched the string of numbers pulse on the screen. She swiped just in time, slowly easing the phone to her ear.

"Hello?" she said with the hint of question, wondering what this woman could possibly have to say. What explanation she had. What truths she had to tell that Amelia needed so desperately to hear.

"You have no idea how long I've wanted to hear your voice," A thick Australian accent came across the speaker. "We've been looking for you for years, darling."

The voice sounded young. Much younger than she expected, as caution and suspicion overtook her excitement. If this was someone's idea of a trick, it was certainly a cruel one.

The voice continued, as Amelia searched for how to answer. "I know you must be confused. You must have so many questions," she said.

"I have hundreds, actually," Amelia said, on guard and slightly peeved.

"And I'm ready to answer them," the woman on the other end of the phone said. "At least the ones I can."

"Where did you drop me, when you decided you didn't want me?" Amelia let her anger slip through just a bit, as she waited again.

"At the hospital in Houston, just outside the sliding doors. Snuggled in a white blanket and tucked into a basket. We made sure you were safe before we left. And you were not unwanted. Not one bit. I never wanted to let you go. But it was for the good of us all," she explained.

"You're not making any sense," Amelia said, wishing the woman on the phone would stop talking in riddles. "Who are '*we*'?"

"I need you to come home Amelia. Home to Australia. It's time you rejoined the Colony," she said.

The next day she put in her vacation request and three weeks later, found herself at the airport in Perth. Ready to meet a woman she'd always wondered about, and to find the answers she needed.

Amelia looked at her phone, still re-reading the texts from the woman who claimed to be her mother. The pictures she sent must have been from a while ago. The vague and confusing explanations all ran through her mind as she sat.

Finally, the pilot came over the speaker, announcing the time, asking all passengers to stay seated until the seatbelt light was turned off.

Even the direct flight had taken nearly an entire day. An entire day spent sitting on a plane. Even with the first-class treatment it was still an entire day spent sitting on a plane.

Amelia was irritated as she walked down the ramp. The time change was messing with her mind. And she was minutes away from meeting the woman who dumped her at a hospital shortly after she was born.

She didn't know what to expect, but at the same time, if this turned out to be a shit-show, she had two full weeks to discover the land down under. She'd make the most of her time, regardless.

When she stepped into the terminal, she spotted her name on a card. Walking up to the strange man, she introduced herself. "I'm Amelia," she huffed. He flashed a bright smile, then bowed. "I'm so happy to meet you, Ma'am. I'm Trevor. Let's see about your luggage," he said, grabbing her carry on without asking.

She followed him through the terminal, thankful that he knew where they were going at least. She looked at the other people around her, passing by, lost in their own thoughts and plans. She noticed their attire was drastically different than hers. The light tank top layered with a cardigan and shorts she wore said to her that she was slightly underdressed.

Leaving Texas in July it was nearing 100 degrees in the early afternoons. She'd packed light, cool clothing.

From what she knew about Australia, it was just as hot as Texas, but covered in dusty deserts and filled with kangaroos.

"Excuse me, why do I get the feeling I misjudged my outfit?" she asked Trevor, who grinned good-naturedly at her question.

"Because it's about 11 degrees outside today. Celsius," he said with a laugh. "Don't worry, Miss. Your mother has a suitcase for you in the car."

"She's not my mother," Amelia shot back. "She's . . . I don't know what she is."

"Apologies. Miss. Phoebe has taken care of your wardrobe. She has excellent taste," he said.

Mentioning Phoebe as her mother made her think. What would she call this woman? This person who for all purposes, did have the title of being her mother. If only in a biological sense. But nevertheless, her mother.

Even though she did drop her off at a hospital when she was days old, just to seek her out after 25 years and beg her to come home to Australia, half a world away. Her mind continued to spiral as they walked.

Would she be offended to be called Phoebe, or even Mrs. Alura? She didn't want to offend the woman, but yet again, she couldn't think of a title that felt comfortable to her yet.

Trevor was nice enough to pick up her suitcase filled with useless clothing from the carousel, wheeling it through the throngs of people, and into the chilly outside air. At least the sun was shining, she thought.

She continued to follow her escort to a long black limousine parked along the curb, in the reserved area at the terminal entrance, which only further piqued her curiosity. Was Phoebe trying to make an impression, or did she have this kind of money? The questions only mounted on her already long list.

They must have been in a hurry, or late. Trevor nearly threw her case and bag into the trunk, then hurried her into the car, running around to the driver's side and flinging himself inside. "All set Miss," he said brightly. "Window up or down, Miss?" he asked.

"Oh, down is fine. And please, call me Amelia," She could tell he was trying to be polite, but they could skip formalities. They were about the same age, from what she could tell. And she wasn't sure how to respond to the over the top treatment he was giving her.

"Sure thing Amelia. Your, uh, Phoebe is waiting for you at one of the best restaurants in town. I hope you're hungry," he said.

"I'm starved and still chilly. Did you mention something about warm clothes?" she asked with a grin.

"Yes Ma'am. I'll turn up the heat. And they're in the suitcase right behind me. I'll put up the window to give you some privacy to change," he said, raising the blackout partition window. In fact the entire car was blackout windows she noticed, as she groped for a switch, turning on the overhead dome light.

She drug the suitcase toward her, with a bit of effort. There must be a ton of things in there. Apparently shopping was a favorite activity of Phoebe's. Either that or she figured that Amelia would come unprepared, which irked her for some reason.

Unzipping the top, she saw a carefully packed trove of pants and sweaters, along with a pair of black combat or hiking boots, which seemed odd, considering they were going into town.

Amelia shrugged. It wasn't her idea of fashion, but then again, what did she know about Australian fashion anyway? She chose a pair of jeans and a deep green sweater along with a pair of socks for the boots.

She kept her back turned to the front of the limo as she quickly stripped, piece by piece, and put on her new clothes. They fit perfectly. Together they looked nice, and most importantly, she was warm now, thank God.

They made the drive in under ten minutes, which had barely given her enough time to change, let alone think. She felt the limousine start to slow as she looked out the heavily tinted windows at the massive hotel that towered into the sky. "We're at a hotel," she said flatly, as Trevor rolled down the window to the back an inch or two.

"Yes, Ma'am. Miss Phoebe wasn't sure if you'd want to stay with her or have a place of your own, so she reserved the penthouse for you. I'll bring your bags up to your room for you, while you get to know Miss Phoebe in the restaurant downstairs whenever you're ready."

"I'm good," Amelia said, throwing her light clothes in the suitcase and zipping it back up.

Again he darted out of the front, running to the back for her personal luggage and opening her door while grabbing the suitcase from inside. She took her time getting out and looking around, then noticed how uncomfortable Trevor looked as he waited impatiently for her to come inside.

She supposed there would be plenty of time for sight-seeing. She'd be here for two full weeks. Walking up the to the hotel, Trevor darted past her, opening the door wide for her, then following right behind. Inside the building, under the florescent lights, she saw the reason for Trevor's discomfort.

The skin on his arm had darkened in blotches, some kind of reaction to the sun she guessed. At once she felt bad. If he had told her, she wouldn't have dawdled. But, by the time they had checked in at the front, the spots had already begun to fade.

"Thank you so much for the ride, Trevor," she said. "Which way to the restaurant?" she asked, instantly nervous again at the thought of meeting the woman who claimed to be her mother.

Trevor pointed directly behind her. "Just through there, Miss. I'll have your things in your room, and here is the key card." He handed over the white plastic card, as she slipped it into her back pocket. With a swift nod or half-bow, he excused himself to the elevator banks just off the main lobby.

She was stalling. She was nervous. Incredibly nervous, and scared. Now or never, she said to herself, putting one foot in front of the other, and heading toward the hallway. Café LuLu was, from the outside, quite an elegant place for a hotel restaurant.

The hostess opened the door wide to an empty room. Empty except for one table by the window. "Welcome Amelia." The hostess greeted her by name, showing her into the dining room.

Either this was an elaborate set-up, or she was being put on some kind of creepy reality TV show.

The woman at the table looked wrong. She looked . . . young. Too young. The two women looked nearly identical. So similar, it forced Amelia to blink against the bright light, questioning whether or not she was imagining things.

They had the same curly dark brown hair and light blue eyes. The same nose and the same high cheekbones. The only difference being their skin color. Amelia had the pale skin she'd always hated. While her mother's skin was a deep brown tan, which only accentuated her eyes more.

Surely this was a joke, she thought as she forced herself to walk closer to the woman at the table.

The woman stood and held her arms wide open for a hug. Amelia offered her hand instead, which evoked little if any emotional response, she noticed. Her mother politely shook her hand instead, retaining her stoic face.

"It's so nice to finally meet you, Amelia. Would you like to take a seat?" her mother asked, gesturing to the table. Amelia picked the chair directly across from her twin and much to her frustration, could not seem to stop staring. The resemblance was uncanny. Spooky. And it reeked of a scam.

"How old are you?" Amelia asked candidly. Her mother giving her a smile, not unnerved or shocked at all by the question. In fact she seemed entertained by it, prepared for it.

"How old do you think I am?" she asked.

"You look about as old as me, which seems impossible considering that you're claiming to be my birth mother. So, if this is a joke, just tell me now, and I'll use my time here doing something fun, then take my free ticket and go back home," she said, making a move to stand from the table.

"I am your mother," She said in a soft voice, trying to be convincing. "And I'm 63 years old. And I don't for a minute expect you to believe me, so. . . ." The woman stared at Amelia, holding her captive with a stare, as she felt something strange shift in her mind, thoughts being moved, and feelings being created.

Immediately and for no reason whatsoever, she instantly trusted the woman across the table from her. Knew that she was telling the truth, and felt deep inside that she would not hurt her or lie to her. She didn't understand how she knew, she just . . . knew.

"I believe you," Amelia told her.

"I know all of this is odd, to say the least. But I promise you that by the end of today you'll have a better understanding of who I am, who we are, and most importantly, who you are. I promise to tell you everything I can.

"You are here as a guest. *Our* guest and you can leave any time you wish. You can say no to anything. But we do need you and you *are* special Amelia. More special than you can imagine," her mother said, reaching out and placing her hand over her daughter's. Her gentle and soothing tone helping to put Amelia even more at ease.

"Can I ask, why am I so important? And, if I'm so damned important, why did you leave me at a hospital when I was only a few days old?" Amelia asked, her emotions warring inside her mind. Anger and sadness were fighting for control. But something was keeping them controlled. In check.

"I can tell that you're unsure of how to feel right now. And that's ok. I've been nervous these past few months too. I mean, how can you explain something like this?

"I can tell you that leaving you in Houston was the hardest thing I've ever had to do. Letting you grow up apart from the Colony, letting you be free to be yourself. But it was absolutely necessary." She paused, letting Amelia take in everything she was saying.

"The Colony . . .?" Amelia led off as a question.

"We are a community. A family. We're special and unique, like you. And in two days you'll join us for the Celebration, learning more about *us* and your background," her mother said brightly. "Would you mind if I asked you some questions?" her mother continued.

"Of course," she replied and waited.

"Let's move away from the window first," she said standing and bringing her cup of tea along with her. They moved to a table in the corner, in the shadows. "Watch closely," her mother said, as they sat in silence.

Amelia stared, watching her mother's skin slowly, very slowly, start to blotch in the same way Trevor's had. The

15

deep tan was now a mottled white and brown pattern on her arm, which traveled to her face.

"Don't be frightened, I can feel it changing, so I know you can see it too," she said in a calm voice.

Five minutes later her mother's skin had lightened to the same pale complexion Amelia had naturally. "How? Wait, I saw the same thing, for a second earlier. With Trevor," Amelia said.

"It's a trait our bloodline shares," she said. "Did you, do you, burn quickly when you're in the sun for too long?"

"I do. I have to wear sunblock all the time or I turn red. Not tan, like you," she answered.

"And your eyes. They're blue like mine. Do you have problems with light sensitivity, even inside?"

"How do you know all of this?" Amelia asked.

"Because we do too. Our entire bloodline. Before we are Unbound, and still human, we have things that make us different and unique already. I expected you to be the same in some ways, maybe different in others." She tried to explain in that same esoteric way that left Amelia slightly frustrated.

"I feel calm when I should be freaking out. Why am I so calm? And what do you mean Unbound?"

"Do you feel things deeply? Know what other people are thinking and feeling just by their demeanor, or by the way they look. Are you sensitive? Do you pick up on things that others don't?"

"Yes," Amelia said, waiting for the next question.

"I do too. You're most likely an empath, like me. That's why I could reach into your mind and influence your emotions and your thoughts so easily. I can influence you to feel things, or not feel things. Like convincing you to feel a certain way, without using words. Just now I influenced you to feel like you could trust me, that I'm telling you the truth, and that I would never hurt you."

"Okay, I can't do that. At least I don't think I can."

"No, not while you're still bound to your mortal self. It's a lot to explain, and there are a lot of unbelievable things still to come. But I promise you that very soon, you'll understand everything." She winked, as she sipped her tea again.

They ordered lunch as Amelia continued to ask questions. Most of which were promised to be answered later. She did make sure though to ask about her father.

"I will tell you this. Within the Colony, we have laws. Rules that must be observed. Most importantly, the men of our tribe can only have children with Unbound women.

"And before a woman can Unbind, she must bear two children, to keep the bloodline growing. I had already had Michelle and Robert before I met your father." She looked down. A flash of sadness crossing her face.

"He was from a different bloodline. You are something special, my darling. Something unique. Something that could change the Colony. That's why my special girl, it was time for you to come home."

A BRIEF STAY IN LUXURY

Amelia and her mother finished their lunch and their conversation. Which most anyone would agree won the prize for "strangest mother-daughter first time conversation ever." The list of questions only kept growing in Amelia's mind, as they made their way up to the penthouse.

"Why did it take you so long to find me, if you've been looking this whole time? I live less than an hour from the hospital you dropped me at," Amelia asked with a sharp edge.

"Because when I left you there, I had no idea what might happen. I only knew that you were safe. I watched the nurse come to the door and gather you up. From there I had no idea what name you'd been given, or where you had gone. Amelia is a lovely name by the way," she said as the doors to the elevator slid open and Amelia unlocked the door to her room.

It was gorgeous. A stunning view of the ocean could be seen through a wall of windows, the water glinting with the sun as boaters came and went from the marina. If she looked down for too long, she started getting a bit light-headed.

"Well, since you asked," Amelia snapped, "I bounced from foster home to foster home after you left me. Which isn't as fun as it sounds. After that I finally got adopted into a family that didn't really care that much about me. I moved out at 17, put myself through community college, and worked my ass off to buy a home of my own."

"You're resourceful and strong. I admire that," Phoebe said, trying to play nice.

"Yeah, well what's done is done I guess," Amelia said, dismissing the conversation.

"Well, Trevor has all your bags in the closet, and you're free to order room service *anytime* you'd like. I highly recommend the breakfast here, and the spa downstairs," Phoebe said, walking toward the window, joining her daughter.

"So, you're rich?" Amelia asked bluntly.

"The Colony members pay 'dues' of a sort. And yes, we have money. Each member of the colony has responsibilities to achieve before they are Unbound. A college education, two children from our bloodline, and the ceremony itself. But the legacy of the colony has endured for centuries and has amassed quite a portfolio," she grinned.

"So, what's the whole bloodline thing about you keep talking about? And centuries, hu? What is it like a secret society or something?"

"In a way, yes. Our lineage begins hundreds of years ago. The history of our kind goes back for thousands of years. And yes, we have to maintain a secrecy for our own protection. Nearly every culture on the planet has some version of us in their legends.

"When New Holland was colonized in 1788, we chose to come to this new and unknown land along with others of a different bloodline, in an attempt to escape the radical religious persecution that threatened us all in Europe at the time."

"I still don't understand. What does it mean to be 'Unbound'? Am I a part of the Colony? Am I Unbound? And what needs to be kept a secret?" Amelia rambled on question after question.

"Would you like to go for a walk outside, see the marina, and get some fresh air? We can talk more, and you can see the sights."

"I'm sure I'll have plenty of time for that."

"Actually, we will be heading out day after next, so you can see the Colony for yourself, and meet the rest of your family. It won't be as luxurious as this, I can assure you. And we'll be there for about a week. Which is why I have to give you such a stark and shortened version of everything. Believe me, I wish we had more time to talk. We should take advantage of the time we have now before we leave."

"Why for so long?" Amelia asked. "What's happening the day after tomorrow?"

"Our Corroboree Celebration, which is an event we hold twice a year. Unbinding and other rituals. It's something of a spectacle, especially for someone who's never been before," she briefly explained.

"And that's why the crash course? Because I have to be honest. It's not making a lot of sense right now," Amelia said.

"The more we talk, the more sense it will make. And seeing the Celebration will help you understand a lot more than I could ever explain. But I'd like to show you the city while we have time, and get some fresh air," her mother suggested again.

"I'd like to see the water . . . I guess"

"Let's go then."

Once they exited the rear of the hotel Phoebe stood in the sun, in a secluded spot for a few minutes, as Amelia watched her skin begin to acclimate to the sun. Soon, she became the same deep tan she had been when they first met.

"That is so weird," Amelia said, as her mother stepped out into the open, giving her a look of slight disapproval.

"It's the melanin in our skin. It protects us from burning. Over the generations, our bodies have developed ways to protect themselves. Another important and beneficial result of expanding the Colony. Introducing new ethnicities and cultures into our bloodline helped us evolve over time."

"What do you mean?" Amelia asked.

"When we first came here, this place was an island prison for the undesirable people of Europe. But over time more people came to the land, and we accepted them into the colony. We are highly diverse you'll find," Phoebe said with a smile.

They picked their way down the stairs leading to the water's edge. A wide walking trail surrounded the marina, bikers and joggers sped by them as they enjoyed their leisurely stroll.

"You asked me earlier about Unbinding," her mother said, receiving a nod from Amelia.

"Unbinding is a ritual. It's permitted only after the criteria I mentioned earlier have been met. It's a custom thousands of years old. It means that you are released from your mortality, simply. More complicated, it also means that the human restrictions you've been bound by are no longer an issue.

"And no, you are not Unbound by simply being of our bloodline. You must be included in the ritual, one that is performed only twice a year, thus the Corroboree Celebration. Because you were removed from the Colony at birth, you are exempted from the conditions for Unbinding. After learning more about it, it's your decision about whether or not you wish to join us."

"What do you mean, join you?" Amelia asked.

A man traveling toward them, slowed, addressing her mother. "Good Afternoon," he said bowing briefly, which confused Amelia. She remembered Trevor doing the same to her this morning.

"Is this....?" he trailed off, glancing at Amelia then bowing to her in the same simple way. Okay now this was weird, she thought.

"It is. And yes, she will be joining us at the Celebration. But, please Hendrick, keep this between us?" She asked the deeply tanned man.

"Yes Ma'am, of course." He bowed again. Another question for another time. "I will let you two get back to your day. A pleasure to finally meet you, Amelia," he said to her, then bowed again before picking up speed and jogging on his way.

"What the hell was that all about? How did he know my name?" Amelia asked. Forgetting her last question completely.

"Word travels in our community. I told you that you were special. The Colony has been waiting twenty-five years for you to come home. Hendrick was there when you were born," she said.

"And he's Unbound too?" Amelia asked.

"Yes. We prefer the term Garkain to describe what we are. Unbinding is only the process of becoming Garkain. Keep a watchful eye. We're everywhere. In every walk of life. On every continent. We're all around you," she said. "It's essential that we blend into normal society. Maintain jobs, go about life in a normal way. But knowing what you do now, you'll be able to tell our kind from others."

"Others, you mean humans?" Amelia said a little too loudly, glancing around.

"Yes." Her mother said in a clipped tone. A hint that Amelia should be more aware of her volume and public questions in the future.

"Even in the States?" Amelia asked, curious now.

"Yes, but there are other groups around the world, other Colonies and communities like our own. Our Colony has its own rules, its own laws. And we're also the only one that I know of that can co-exist with our neighbors," Phoebe said in that same vague and frustrating way she had everything else.

They turned a corner traveling down one of the side streets, Phoebe making sure to stay in the shadows for a bit while her skin began to pale. Small shops and cafes, including a coffee shop which caught Amelia's eye. "Can we grab a coffee?" she asked.

"Of course, whatever you'd like." Her mother smiled as they went in and placed their orders. Amelia watched as she stared in concentration at the barista behind the counter, who made their drinks then handed them over without asking for payment.

"That is such a cool trick," Amelia said.

"One of the things about the human body is that they are limited by natural laws. Once you Unbind, those laws don't apply any longer. The aging process stops, your strength and your mind are enhanced, in a way. The natural things that make you who you are, are simply magnified, enhanced. Many different gifts are found within the Colony. Some share the same ones, as I expect you will share mine."

Amelia nodded and sipped the latte, a nice warm cup in her cold holds. She was learning quite a bit, putting together the pieces. As strange as the pieces were. But the picture was still very broken and in need of more information. Information that Phoebe was intentionally leaving out for some reason.

"Shall we head back to the hotel? You look cold," her mother suggested, as Amelia agreed. She was nearly shaking.

The clothes that her mother had packed were warm, but when the wind picked up, it cut right through her sweater. She made a mental note to ask for a coat or pick one up at one of the shops they'd just passed.

"And to answer the last question. You are a part of the Colony. You're linked through blood, but that doesn't mean you have to join us. I want to stress that the decision is yours entirely, Amelia. Whatever you decide, we *will* understand."

They continued back to the water, watching again as the ships came and went. Fishing boats and large yachts made their way in and out as she watched.

"Aren't you cold?" she asked her mother, noticing that she was dressed just the same as Amelia, yet she never seemed to shiver.

"Another perk of being Unbound, neither the heat nor the cold bothers you. We can feel it a little, but not in the same way you do."

"You make it sound great. Why do you make it so clear that I have the choice to say no. Why would anyone say no?" Amelia pushed.

"Because with every perk, there comes a drawback. A balance to things. And danger. Our kind is misunderstood. A lot of bad press in various forms. You'll see. For now, though, let's enjoy the rest of the afternoon."

Amelia continued to process and think as they strolled. "I've wondered about my biological history for so long, and now there's so much to take in all at once. All the things I had imagined growing up were so far from reality," Amelia said with a laugh.

"I wish there was more time to ease you gently into all of this. I truly do. But I had to tell you in this way because of time constraints. Like ripping off the band-aid, so to speak. You must attend the Celebration, and I wanted to have the time to talk with you and explain at least a few things before you arrived. To prepare you," her mother said.

"As fantastic as this all sounds, and as shocking as it is to hear. Without a bit of understanding, the Celebration would have been overwhelming if you were to just dive in," Phoebe continued to explain.

Amelia stifled a yawn. Despite the coffee and the conversation, the long day had crept up on her.

It was getting late in Australia, but in America, it was nearly time for her to wake up. Her mind and her body were more than a little confused at the moment. She had a feeling that tonight would be a tough night for sleeping. Especially considering all the information she would be processing as she tossed and turned. Her mind already had trouble letting go and calming down at night. And she could only imagine the racing thoughts she'd have running through there now.

They made it quickly through the lobby and into the elevator, scanning the room card which took them to the penthouse floor. Amelia tossed her empty coffee cup into the trash bin by the front door as they walked in, then took a flying leap onto the bed.

Her mother gracefully followed, sitting beside her. Amelia sat up and curled her legs underneath her. "So, I don't think I can sleep tonight. It's like the exact opposite time in the morning in America. Tell me more about the ceremony, tell me more about everything," Amelia asked excitedly.

"There's only so much I can tell you, and so much more that I can show you. Like I said already, seeing is better. You'll understand more then. Would you like me to help you sleep? I can if you'd like," she offered.

"You mean, do that hypnosis thing? I think I'll pass. I might stay up for a bit."

"Well, take the day tomorrow to relax and get some rest. You'll need it. And take my advice on breakfast and the spa. Trust me," her mother said smiling.

"I will," Amelia promised. "One more thing though. My Father. Will he be there at the Ceremony?" Amelia pressed for more information.

"No. Your father left us, just after you were born," she said.

"What do you mean left us?" Amelia asked.

"He was killed."

FOUR OF A KIND

"Killed? Okay, you can't say something like that and just think that this conversation is over. I need you to explain," Amelia demanded.

Something was happening inside her mind, some kind of veil lifting. Emotions of confusion, disbelief, outright fear, and anxiety flooded her all at once.

"Remember to stay calm," her mother urged.

"Calm? You want me to be calm?" Amelia pulled herself back onto the bed as her mother tried to catch her gaze. "And no more messing with my head!" she said as she realized her mind was clearing from whatever her mother had done earlier.

"Oh my God," Amelia whispered.

"You're fighting it. Don't do this Amelia. Please try and stay calm. Please . . ." Her mother pleaded with her.

"You're a . . . And you're in charge somehow. And I'm special, because why? Why can I fight through the mind control or hypnosis or whatever? Why did you kill my father?" She rambled off all her questions in a fit of verbal anxiety.

"And you give me two days. Two whole days to come to terms with all this? Two days to process, and then what? I turn into one of you?" Amelia began raising her voice as she got up from the bed, pacing in front of the window.

"You're crazy," she said pointing at her mother, who sat calmly while listening. "And vampires or Garkain, or whatever aren't real. Look, I don't have any money, and I'm not interested in becoming your best friend. If this is some kind of reality show, you got me good. I don't know what you want from me, but I don't believe you, and I'm leaving."

Amelia began to walk toward the closet to grab her things as her mother struggled to calm her down.

"We are called Garkain. We're very much real, and everything I'm telling you is the truth I swear! Please, Amelia. Look, look," her mother begged as she opened her mouth. Amelia watched as two sharp canines grew from *behind* her original teeth.

"Holy shit," she gasped as she kept moving toward the closet and the bathroom, putting as much space as she could between this woman and herself.

"You're special and you can fight my influence because your father was a Larougo. A lycanthrope. You're both Amelia," her mother said pausing. Letting her have a minute to process.

"That's why he was killed, that's why you were sent away, and that's why you're so damned special!" her mother said frantically, tears coming into her eyes.

Amelia stopped. She believed her. Kind of. To be honest, at this point she didn't know what the hell to believe.

"I fell in love. Not the mating rituals of the Colony, but actual love. When you were born, the Larougo pack considered the same fate for you as for your father.

"Yes, I am someone inside the Colony. Your great-great-grandfather is one of the original Garkain who fled Europe in 1788. I am a Duchess, and you are a Countess. *You* are Garkain royalty. And it's only because of that, that I was able to strike a bargain.

"I let you go. They made me let you go. I left you at that hospital in Houston to save your life! To prove that without knowing what you were, you would live a normal life. And once you'd proven that, you would be brought back home. We searched for years in the beginning. But for all the money and the gifts we had, we couldn't find you. Not until the DNA test.

"But we needed to know who you were. As a person without any knowledge of our kind. Do you understand?"

"No, I don't." Amelia's eyes narrowed in anger at her mother on the bed. "It all sounds crazy. Like you're delusional and you need to see a psychiatrist," Amelia shot back at her mother, more than a little leery of her.

"What more do I have to do to convince you? I've shown you my skin, the way it changes in the light. I've shown you my teeth, which I think you'd agree aren't normal. The only thing I have left is to show you the Colony in person, to let you talk to others. Like Trevor and the man you saw jogging today.

"Yes, we drink blood. But we never take a human life. It's forbidden. A cause for culling. And we have no idea what will happen if you choose to Unbind. The Larougo can resist our influence, that's why you're reacting to all of this now. All of a sudden. Please, Amelia, calm down. You fought your way through it, and this is all hitting you at once."

"I don't *want* to calm down. Do you think a normal person is just supposed to just accept all of this? I come here, expecting to find out where I came from. Why I was *tossed* away. And then I meet you, who hypnotizes me or whatever, and I'm supposed to be ok with that? Then I'm told I'm part vampire, part werewolf bloodline, and I'm supposed to be cool with that too? What else is there? Can I shoot laser beams out of my eyes or see through walls?"

Amelia was having difficulty breathing, her chest heaving as she hyperventilated. This was all terrifying, and unbelievable, but true. That's the one thing she couldn't deny. It *was* all true. Her mother had proved that beyond a shadow of a doubt. She wasn't normal. Her mother was far, far from normal.

She took a few deep breaths, processing what to say next, as her mother patiently waited on the bed. "Don't do that mind thing to me again. Promise me that," Amelia demanded.

"I promise. Not unless you ask me to."

"Okay. Okay." Amelia repeated, still making sense of everything.

"I believe you. I believe what you're telling me and what you showed me, but I have some questions of my own.

About me. There's always been something different about me. I've always known it. That's one of the biggest reasons I wanted to meet you. So you could explain why I am the way I am. So, just give it to me straight."

"I have so far, haven't I?" her mother asked, making a good point.

"You already explained the sun thing. That's why I can never tan, right?" Her mother nodded in response. "I can smell things, like things that no one else can, and see really well in the dark. I'm guessing that part comes from my father?"

"I would dare to guess that you're correct. But we really are only speculating at this point."

"And the hearing thing?"

"Hearing noises far away, and being sensitive to loud noises? Jumpy even."

"Also a Larougo trait, but a Garkain one too." Her mother kept patiently answering her.

"Why are you dodging my questions? Why can't you give me a straight answer?" Amelia asked.

"Because my dear girl, you are the first child of a Larougo and Garkain that's been allowed to survive in our Colony," her mother said with gravity.

"What do you mean?"

"I mean that you weren't supposed to be allowed to live. And as far as what to expect or the questions you have, no one can answer them here, because the answer is, we simply don't know."

"This is all so confusing. My head is spinning," Amelia said, dropping into one of the overstuffed chairs by the kitchen. "So what happens now?" she asked, terrified of what could possibly be coming next.

"Now, you get some rest. If you'd like, I can stay in the living space, on the pull out couch," her mother said gently.

"Yeah. I mean, yes, please. I'm kind of freaking out *just a little*," Amelia snapped.

"Not a problem at all. I'll be in the other room if you need anything. Just wake me up and let me know."

"Wait don't . . . Garkain stay up all night, or need a coffin or something?" Amelia shyly asked.

Her mother laughed loudly, making Amelia smile. "Oh my darling girl, you watch too many movies! Get some sleep. I'll take care of breakfast, and we'll both treat ourselves to a day at the spa. How does that sound?"

Amelia was calming down now, a little. "Sounds pretty good actually."

She kicked off her shoes, and changed into her comfy nightclothes in the closet, as she heard her mother pulling out the bed in the living room.

She pulled back the soft sheets and sunk into the big bed, willing her mind to turn off, to stop thinking. It had been one hell of a day, to say the least. And from what her mother said, things were about to get even stranger. If that were even possible.

It wasn't a shock that sleep was hard to find. Between the time difference and all the crazy thoughts running through her head, she couldn't shut her mind off, no matter how hard she tried. At some point though, she must have slept for a bit at least.

The next morning Amelia awoke to the smell of coffee and something else. In a sleepy haze, she stumbled into the full kitchen, seeing an assortment of breakfast items. Her mouth watered as her eyes glanced over the offerings. Pancakes, eggs, bacon, and coffee. God, did she need some coffee.

She sat at the table, pilling her plate high and digging in, looking for Phoebe, who wasn't in the living room when she passed by a minute ago.

She heard the door to the restroom open and glanced over to see her mother fresh from the shower, and in new clothes. She must have had someone bring them, Amelia thought. Trevor probably.

She stopped mid-chew, stuck for how to start the conversation. She simply stared at her mother, until she finally spoke.

"How did you sleep?" Phoebe asked like today was going to be a normal day, even though the air itself was laden with awkwardness. She was trying to put Amelia more at ease around her, or at least more at ease than she was last night.

"Terribly. My head was spinning all night. Strange dreams. But that's not unusual for me."

"What kind of dreams?" her mother asked, attempting to keep the light conversation going.

Amelia chuckled. "Actually, I had a dream about being stuck inside a rock." She blushed. "People having sex. Just random things."

"Well, that *is* interesting," her mother replied, pouring herself a cup of coffee, but offering nothing else about her dreams, thank goodness.

"Aren't you hungry?" Amelia asked, pilling her plate high with all the tasty offerings as her stomach grumbled in anticipation.

"I already ate. Room service was delicious," she smiled.

"Seriously?" Amelia gaped.

"She's fine. Our saliva has a natural coagulant, the bite seals right up. If you do decide to Unbind, you're going to have to learn how to feed. You can eat regular food too, but it's not what your new body will need," she said, picking up her cup of coffee and sipping it, then adding a bit more sugar.

"You make this all seem so normal," Amelia said, chewing on a bite of an omelet.

"It is mostly, once you get used to it. Not at first. At first, it's a bit of a learning curve. But after a while, you'll learn how to adapt and blend in. Live a semi-normal life. Learning how to use the gift is probably the trickiest part."

"What different kinds of gifts are there? I mean, besides being able to influence people?" Amelia asked.

"Well, our senses are all very keen already as humans, which is typical of anyone from the bloodline, as you already know. But once you Unbind, your mind can expand in ways it never could before. So, for us, as empaths, we can read other's emotions pretty well. So, once you Unbind, you can 'modify' those feelings. Reach inside their minds and make them feel the way you want or need them to, within reason at least.

"Other people have a psychic gift from birth, and once Unbound, they can look into people's subconscious to see what they're thinking, some can see into the future. We're all tuned in to nature, so within reason, we can coexist with it on a different level.

"I am curious to see what your gift will be, but I'm pretty sure you'll be close to me. Which is wonderful, and I can teach you how to use it. Your brother and sister are both empaths as well."

"Oh my God, I completely forgot about them. That's terrible of me, isn't it? We've just had so much to talk about, that it slipped my mind entirely. When do I get to meet them?" Amelia asked.

"They live here in the city if you'd like for us all to have lunch? Or we can wait until the Celebration. I don't want to overexpose you anymore than I already have. Especially after yesterday. I realize now that was too much too soon."

"No, it's fine. I just wish you'd been straight with me instead of influencing me. I don't like being taken advantage of or being made a fool of. Trust is a very big thing with me," Amelia said, making that clear.

"I understand completely. I'm the same. How about we finish breakfast, then head down to the spa? I have us an appointment for a four-hour pampering session, which means we'll be finishing up just about lunchtime. I'll text Robert and Michelle to meet us in the lobby at the same restaurant," she said, already pulling out her phone.

"If that's okay with you . . ." Her mother verified, glancing at Amelia for her permission.

"Yes, absolutely. And tell them I'm in on the whole deal, so no hypnotism from them either," Amelia said.

"They haven't Unbound yet. Being of the royal bloodline, all siblings must Unbind at the same time. We were waiting for you my darling." She smiled across the table, then typed away on her phone.

Amelia suddenly felt pressured. "You've continually said it's my choice, right? What if I say no? What happens to them?"

Her mother sighed. "If you decide against the ritual, you'll be shunned from the Colony. Your memory will be erased, and you will find yourself back home in the States wondering where two weeks of your life went. They will Unbind together and assume their roles. We won't bother you again. I promise. But I do hope that you decide to join us, for what it's worth." She reached across the table patting her daughter's hand in that comforting way she had yesterday at lunch.

Their trip to the spa was, as her mother had promised, heavenly. But her mind refused to stay quiet. Anxiety about lunch, the questions she longed to ask, and the fear over meeting her brother and sister for the first time occupied her thoughts, as she was rubbed and scrubbed.

As they dressed in the changing room, she noticed the time, nearly noon.

"Tell me about Michelle and Robert," Amelia said, as they started out of the spa. She'd like to know more about them before meeting them. Make a good first impression.

"After getting to know you, I'd say you're a lot alike. You and Michelle especially. The way you talk, your mannerisms and expressions. And you'll be surprised by how much you two look alike."

Amelia was even more excited and anxious to meet them now. Growing up she never had a brother or sister until she was adopted as a foster-child, and even then, it wasn't the same thing.

They walked past the front desk and into the restaurant for the second time in two days. Amelia just as nervous as she was yesterday, meeting her mother for the first time. Now, she was about to meet the other part of her family.

This time, however, the restaurant was busy. Either her mother had orchestrated it to be empty for their first visit, or it just happened to be a slow day yesterday. She assumed it was the former.

Amelia scanned the room, looking by the windows first. She didn't see anyone that looked familiar, then turning her head, she spotted a woman about her age, that she recognized instantly.

Like mother, like daughters, she thought. Although they were from separate biological fathers, their mother's genes created a striking resemblance. Michelle stood, noticing Amelia as well. Robert hung back in his seat, seeming a little irritated, as he briefly looked up from his phone.

"I can't believe you're finally here," Michelle said, reaching out and pulling Amelia in for a tight hug. "We have so much to talk about!" Amelia politely tried to extricate herself, without appearing rude. She just wasn't much of a hugger.

"Believe me, I have a lot of questions," Amelia said, awkwardly waiting to be introduced to her sullen brother in the corner.

"This is Robert," Michelle said. "He's in a mood. Which is typical. Just ignore him. I do."

Amelia decided that she was going to get along with Michelle just fine, and she was grateful to have another person to talk to besides her mother, who came off as far more serious than Michelle, who exuded a bubbly personality that Amelia would normally find annoying. But for some reason it fit Michelle perfectly.

"I am not in a mood," Robert bickered with his sister, "I'm hungry. We've been waiting here for over an hour because Michelle has to be early to everything," he said, smirking at his sister, then extending his hand and shaking Amelia's. "It is a pleasure to *finally* meet you," he said, again shooting his sister a look.

"I'm sorry, I thought I told you both we were meeting at noon," their mother stepped in, taking a seat.

Amelia and Michelle sat beside each other, across from their brooding brother. "You did." Michelle said matter of factly. "But, we, sorry, I, didn't want to be late in case you both happened to be early," she said smiling.

"Well, we're all here now, and we can finally order," Robert said, raising his hand for their waiter.

"I'm starving too. And I think I'll have the burger I had yesterday," Amelia said, smiling at Robert, trying to get on his good side, if he had one.

"Do you crave meat sometimes?" Michelle asked, leaning over toward Amelia.

"I do. How did you know?" Amelia asked.

"It's a Garkain thing. Even when you're still Bound, it's like our bodies crave iron all the time. We're big meat-eaters. It could be a Larougo thing too. I'm so excited to see what happens when you Unbind," Michelle said with that same bubbly exuberance, while trying to keep her voice low. She was full of energy this morning, or maybe this was how she always was, Amelia thought.

"Michelle, that's entirely up to Amelia. She's just been introduced to the idea of the Colony and Unbinding. You've both grown up with all of this. Let her adjust. Yesterday was a crash course, which was difficult for her," their mother jumped in.

"Of course, I just mean, if she decides to. I'm curious to see what happens, that's all," Michelle explained. "You're one of a kind, Amelia. When we're done here, do you want to go hang out, grab some coffee?" Michelle asked.

"I'd love to," Amelia said, accepting the invitation. She realized this could be an opportunity to get to know her better, and to ask some questions that she and Michelle could keep private. She also realized that her mother was right. They were very much alike, except for Michelle's energy level. The feeling of kinship was undeniable, the banter flowing easily through lunch, as Robert stayed to himself.

"Amelia, I do have some things to take care of before we head out tomorrow, but I will see you later. In the meantime, you and Michelle enjoy your time together," their mother said.

She and Robert both left, leaving the girls to have the rest of the afternoon for themselves. "So, what do you want to do?" Michelle asked.

"Talk . . . honestly."

"You got it. I'll tell you everything you want to know and answer any questions you have. I can't even imagine what's going on in your head right now," she said with a grin.

"You have no idea!"

GETTING TO KNOW YOU

The two girls sat on the king-size bed in Amelia's penthouse suite, sharing stories of their past. How they both liked the same kind of foods and how similar their tastes were in movies and books. They were warming up to big stuff, but this part was fun too. It only helped to solidify the fact that they were in fact so uncannily alike.

After Amelia was adopted she'd tried to find a common ground with her new siblings, but there was always something missing. She knew now what that was. For her and Michelle it was just easy, they were sisters, as simple as that.

"I know this isn't what you meant when you said you wanted to talk," Michelle finally said. "You don't have to be scared to ask me what you want to know. I grew up going to the Celebrations and all the things that come with being a part of the Colony. It's like being raised in America, it seems so natural to you, but I have a ton of questions for you!" She smiled, trying to put Amelia at ease. "But later," she said, lowering her enthusiasm and allowing Amelia to speak.

"My dad. Do you remember him?" Amelia asked. The one big thing she was missing, was information about him.

Michelle shook her head. "I don't, but I do know the story. If you want to hear it. I can tell you, but it doesn't end well."

"I already know he's . . . gone. But I need to know the rest, and I need to know why I'm so special because of him," Amelia said.

"His name was Lachlean, and yes he was from the Larougo bloodline. A werewolf, as *you* would say. But the Larougo aren't wolves, they're dingos. The wild dogs you see roaming around by day. At night, the Larougo become human. It runs in their blood like Garkain does in ours.

"If we're as alike as I think we are, then we're both independent and strong-willed. We push our boundaries and don't like taking no for an answer or being told what to do. We get that from our mother. She fell in love with Lachlean. She didn't care what happened. But the leader of the Larougo pack was the one who killed your father.

"Because of her status in the Colony, *she* was given a choice. We aren't enemies, Garkain and Larougo. Our truce was struck centuries ago when we first came to Australia. But inter-breeding isn't allowed. Children born of both Garkain and Larougo aren't allowed to survive. So that answers the why you're so special question. Because no Garkain and Larougo children have ever survived in the Colony. Until now."

"That's terrible. Why would they do that?"

"It's not our decision about the children. It's a pack rule for the Larougo. Heavy bargaining needed to be made to save you. Firstly, you had to be given away, know nothing about the Colony, or who we were. To see how your mortal life might be different. Secondly, Lachlean's pack punished him by death. I was too young to remember him. I'm sorry."

"So, we don't have the same father, I'm guessing."

"No, and neither do Robert and I. That's one thing about the Colony, we aren't monogamous. It helps to ensure a variety of different cultural backgrounds and genetics. Although I wasn't required to have children, I decided to. I have two. A boy and a girl, to carry on the royal bloodline. Just as our mother chose to do for us."

Amelia sat for a while mulling over all the information that Michelle had shared with her. One of the biggest questions that remained was, did she want to join the Colony? Stay with her new family and become Unbound. Could she stand by and be a part of a culture that seemed so brutal and antiquated?

All her life she'd wondered what it would be like to find her family, to be a part of their lives. To finally be accepted. And now that she finally had that choice, she wasn't sure if she wanted it or not.

"How do you feel about becoming part of the Colony? Becoming Unbound?" she asked Michelle honestly.

"It's my birthright for one thing. For another, I am a part of the Colony, and so are you, it's in our blood.

Literally. We are exempt from certain obligations because of status, but we're still a part of the Colony. At first, when I began to understand some of our customs and our requirements, the laws and the punishments, it was hard for me to wrap my head around them.

"But I've seen things go very wrong when the rules are broken. The guidelines and rules in place have helped to keep our people safe, and undiscovered. Secrecy is a very important part of who we are. Just bringing you here had to be a process of approvals. But again, being of a certain status, exceptions were made." Michelle patiently explained as Amelia thought of what to ask her sister next.

"What's the best thing about the Colony? What's the best thing about being Unbound?" Amelia asked. Michelle had kept her word. They'd been talking for over an hour and she had answered every question Amelia had come up with. Blunt, with no sugar coating. She began to trust her because of that.

"Wow, I would have to say the feeling of belonging. We would die for each other. Have died for each other. We truly are an unbreakable force together. It's also exciting to be a part of something secret, special. As for being Unbound. I can only tell you what I've seen from my mother and others.

"Immortality first off, with a few exceptions is a plus, at least most of us see it that way. Speed, which is kind of a bummer because the only time we get to practice or have fun with it, is during our gatherings, away from curious human eyes. The same for strength. Then, of course, there's your 'gift'. No one knows exactly what theirs will be, but it's usually something that's already a part of you. Most likely, we'll both be empaths, like our mother."

"Phoebe, mom. You know, I'm still not quite sure what to call her. She said the same thing. That I'll be like her because I can feel other people's emotions, read them already," Amelia said.

Michelle nodded. "That's true. She says the same about me and Robert. It does take some practice to do it right. And you'll have to have a crash course. But from what I've been told, is that for empaths, you feel, deeply. Not about yourself, but the person you're trying to influence. Think deeply about their feelings until you become a part of them. Then you can change how they feel. Shift them around until they fit, or something like that.

"It's not like telling someone to do something or making them do something they don't want to do. You can make them *feel* like they want to do something or feel something you want them to. It's their choice, you just help them feel like making it."

"You make it sound simple. And great, and scary. And I know that if I don't Unbind, neither can you or Robert. Either that or I'm shunned from the family I just met and the Colony. No second chances, which kind of makes me feel pressured," Amelia admitted.

"I could sense that. And we want you to join us, but we, as a society, do respect free will to a certain extent, as long as it doesn't put the Colony or any member at risk. This is your choice. And with enough negotiating, we could come to an agreement. These are special circumstances after all," Michelle said, easing Amelia worry, just a bit.

"About that. If I do Unbind, what do you . . . what do they think will happen?"

Michelle sighed. "We don't know. There are speculations that one side may take over the other. If you chose to undergo the Unbinding ritual, it could make you full Garkain, without any Larougo characteristics at all. Or you may have some combination of the two. Because of the dual bloodlines it's doubtful you would become full lycanthrope or full Garkain. But again, it's all speculation at this point," Michelle explained.

"What about lycanthropes? What about their group?"

Michelle sighed. "We've lived in peace for a long time, as I said before. But it's a strained peace. Larougo and Garkain have a past, and it's one that hasn't always been peaceful. Two different supernatural groups vying for control at one time. Each with their own weapons against the other. Wars raged between us for thousands of years until we came here. For us, we had to learn to coexist or face extinction. So, we came to a place of mutual understanding.

"Larougo can resist our influences completely. They also have poison glands at the base of each claw. The same way we have a coagulant in our saliva. We're stronger, and faster. Physical attributes which have each evolved and changed over time, like our skin. But their venom is toxic. Driving a Garkain mad, and it doesn't end well."

"So Garkain stay as they are, but Larougo can only become human at night. It sounds like nothing I've ever read or heard about."

"Don't believe everything you read or see on TV. And yes, over time we've adapted. And so have they in ways. I've heard that in the beginning they were wolves, but that they adapted into dingos. Which makes more sense. We mostly keep to ourselves, each kind separate. Although Anatole will be there at some point. He's the newest leader of their pack. He wants to see you too. I told you, there's a lot to do about you."

"Now I really am nervous. What if things don't go as well as everyone hopes? Would they kill me?" Amelia couldn't hide the fear in her voice.

"Mother is very powerful, and so is Ambrose, our grandfather. I doubt it would come to that." Amelia could tell that Michelle was trying to ease her worry, but she could also tell that she didn't have all the answers on this one.

"I say, just take it all in tomorrow, see how you feel. And by weeks end, you can make your decision. I'm actually starting to get a little tired, and a little hungry. Mother will be back before night, I'm sure. So we have about an hour left to ourselves. Coffee downstairs and a snack?"

"Sounds like a plan."

They talked a bit more, about less heavy things until, just as the sun was beginning to get lower in the sky, both Amelia and Michelle noticed their mother walking toward their table, sitting down to join them.

"Well, did you two have a nice time?" she asked.

"Absolutely. Amelia and I are like long lost twins. We had a great talk too," Michelle glanced over at Amelia and winked.

"I'm so glad to hear that," she said smiling. "We have a long day ahead of us, as Michelle already knows. And Amelia, I would suggest you take me up on my offer to help you sleep tonight. The planes leave for the Outback at 8:00 A.M. and the Celebration begins at noon," their mother said.

"Are you staying with me again tonight?" Amelia asked.

"If you would like me to, I can."

"I think so, and yes, I will take you up on that offer. I've been dead on my feet all day," Amelia said. "I could use a good night of rest."

"Well, then it's time for you to get home to your family. Your children are driving me crazy, as always," she said to Michelle.

"I know when my time's up," Michelle pouted, then stood and hugged her sister again. "I'll see you in the morning."

"See you in the morning."

Her mother stopped by the front desk, influencing the concierge to have an actual bed brought to the penthouse suite. Amelia guessed the pullout wasn't as comfortable as she thought it would be last night.

Less than an hour later, a knock sounded at the door, with Trevor greeting them both. "Nice to see you again, Miss Amelia. Where would you like your things, Miss Phoebe?" he asked her mother.

"In the front living area. And I'll need your help with both our things in the morning at no later than 6:00," she instructed him curtly, making Amelia flinch.

49

He bowed to them both. "Of course. I will see you in the morning."

As he opened the door, a group of four hotel employees struggled to fit the queen size bed through the elevator opening and set it up in the living area. Amelia watched as they pieced the entire thing together, then made the bed completely and left without a word.

"Ah! So much better." Her mother smiled, pulling down the top covers. "Are you nervous? About tomorrow?" she asked Amelia.

"A little."

Her mother frowned. "Okay, a lot," Amelia admitted.

"Would you like me to help with that too? Take away some of your anxiety? I promise to do only the things you ask me to. And it should wear off by morning. If yesterday gave us an idea of how long my influence will last."

Amelia considered it. Thinking that a nice, stress-free sleep would be heavenly. And that no matter what her mother influenced her mind into thinking or feeling, the effect would be gone by morning.

"Yes. To both. Sleep, and less anxiety. I feel like if you don't, my mind will just spin and spin like last night."

Her mother crossed the room, sitting with Amelia on the bed. "Michelle told me about my father. Lachlean?" Her mother nodded. "I'm sorry. It sounds like you loved him very much. I wish I had the chance to meet him."

"So do I. And yes, I loved him very deeply. And you, my sweet girl, are the only thing I have left of him," she said, gently brushing Amelia's hair behind her back. "Now, I'm going to influence your mind to relax first, and then convince you that you're sleepy. You should be out soon."

"Thanks, mom," Amelia said, finally deciding on what to call the woman she met just yesterday.

"Shhh . . . Just relax."

Within five minutes Amelia began to feel so emotionally light, so relaxed, that she barely needed any help to feel sleepy. It had been anxiety fueling her all day, she realized now. She didn't even remember her head hitting the pillow.

Waking up, she felt refreshed and well rested. The same smell of heavenly coffee with breakfast hit her nose as soon as she opened her eyes. She could certainly get used to this!

"Good morning, how did you sleep?" her mother asked again as Amelia plodded into the kitchen.

"Like a rock. Thank you. I didn't even dream."

"We only have about thirty minutes before Trevor gets here, so eat fast, and get packed. Today you meet the rest of the Colony."

THE COLONY

"I would wear something warm, and the hiking boots. We are taking the plane, but we'll be doing a fair bit of walking too," her mother suggested as Amelia rummaged through her things in the closet.

"What should I do with the rest of my things?" Amelia shouted.

"Leave them, the room is yours for a while, so you'll be back."

A knock at the door and Trevor quickly collected their bags for the trip. They'd be staying at the Colony for a full week, her mother had said. So, they would need to bring several things with them. Toiletries, of course, and a few changes of clothing. From what she understood, this would be similar to a camping trip. Kind of.

Everything else would be pretty unexpected, Amelia guessed. She'd already asked so many questions and received so many answers that she had a basic understanding of the situation. As far as the Celebration was concerned, she took Michelle's advice to just wait and see.

She couldn't help being excited, and nervous. It wasn't what she had planned to be doing when she got on the plane to Australia only a few days ago. Meet your biological family, sure no problem. Become part of a secret Garkain society. As a royal bloodline. And oh yeah, you're half lycanthrope by the way. No big deal, right?

"Amelia, we need to hurry," her mother shouted, as she threw the last few things she might need into a light bag.

"Okay, all set!" she yelled. Seconds later, Trevor was in front of her, collecting her things and taking them out, while she darted to the bathroom one last time.

"Are you ready?" her mother asked, grabbing her hands and looking into her daughter's eyes.

"I think so."

"Then let's get going. We do have time to stop and grab a coffee before the flight if you'd like," her mother offered as she smiled.

"Only if the plane has a bathroom."

"It does," her mother grinned.

A quick stop at LuLu's downstairs and they were heading to the airport, Amelia still nervous. Maybe the extra shot of espresso she ordered wasn't such a great idea after all. Twenty minutes later and they arrived at a much smaller airport than the one she touched down at when she first arrived on the big jet.

Rows of small shiny jets were lined up on the tarmac here, with lots of people waiting and talking. Amelia's social anxiety immediately reared its ugly head.

"I need a favor," she said to her mother in the back of the limousine.

"Okay."

"Can you take away the anxiety again? I'm starting to freak out a little," she asked as her heart began to race and her breathing sped up.

"I can if that's what you want. But this time I'm going to suggest you reconsider. If you decide to Unbind, your senses will all be stronger. Magnified. It will be uncomfortable at first. Maybe even scary, and I'll have no way to help, other than to just be there with you as you go through it. The Colony prohibits the use of influencing on other members. Even if you ask."

"Then one last time, before that happens," Amelia pleaded.

"Before it *happens*? So, you've decided already?" her mother asked, smiling, and obviously happy to hear she was leaning toward joining them after all.

"After talking with Michelle, I think my answer is yes. I've never known a real family. And I can't let her or Robert down. I owe it to them and the Colony. This was always supposed to be my life anyway, right?"

Her mother nodded. "If I had my way, you never would have left us to begin with," her mother said smiling.

"I'm so nervous though, about the whole thing. So, just one last time?" Amelia begged again.

"Okay, my darling," her mother said, reaching into Amelia's mind as she relaxed almost instantly. She was accepting it, she could tell. She could feel it, how it was easier to let her mother in if she knew to expect it. The more she trusted her, the more she opened up.

"Better?"

"Yes, thank you," Amelia said, taking a deep relaxing breath.

"Enough stalling," her mother joked, "It's time to meet everyone."

They stepped onto the private runway, her mother's skin slowly attaining that deep tan that the others on the tarmac already had. She didn't need to acclimate or wait, being around the others she was less inhibited already.

Amelia could hear the distant but indistinct conversations, with gazes directed toward them both. She could both feel and see their eyes on her, as she imagined what they might be saying.

Her mother boldly strode toward the group, some greeting her with deep reverent bows, others with a shake of her hand. From behind her, Amelia heard the sound of tires on the pavement, and a familiar voice, calling out.

"Hey, you!" Michelle shouted. "You two, come and meet your Aunt Amelia," she said to the two children climbing out of the limousine after her.

Amelia bent down, crouching. "Hi you two, it's so nice to meet you," she said to her niece and nephew. They were both button cute and very quiet, she noticed.

"This is Roderick, and this is Camille. Roderick is thirteen and Camille is twelve," she said making introductions.

The two children both stepped forward and extended a hand for Amelia to shake. "So polite, both of you. Are you excited about today?" she asked, hoping their response would make her feel more at ease. They both nodded emphatically but still they stayed quiet.

"It's their first time at the Celebration too. Twelve is the earliest you can attend, and last year Roderick was sick. So you three are all first time participants," she said.

For some reason that put Amelia even more at ease, on top of her mother's influence. If it was a kid-friendly event, she should have nothing to worry about. Or so she hoped.

"Let's go get this part over with. I know you're dreading it," she said, grabbing Amelia's hand and gently dragging her toward the throng of people mingling.

All attention turned to the foursome as they started walking. Michelle, thankfully, stepped in front of Amelia and made the first introduction.

"The girl we've all been waiting for. My sister Amelia." Again, a difference in greetings, deep bows greeted her, while she shook hands with those who offered them. Each person politely saying their hellos. Then slowly, to her relief, they began taking up their previous socializing among themselves.

"See, that wasn't so bad," Michelle whispered into her ear. Amelia smiled.

"Time to go everyone! Let's get the show on the road," a man announced from the door of the lead plane, earning shouts of excitement from the crowd.

"That's Ambrose. He's our leader. And he also happens to be our great-great-grandfather. He's the Prince of the Garkain," she said with pride.

"Who's the King?"

"It doesn't go that far, it's not a true monarchy, it's more of a democracy, but certain individuals, like us, have a bit more pull, if you want to think of it that way. It's really just a title. We have a council that makes the big decisions and all the rules. But of course, some opinions carry more weight than others. He was the one who pushed his weight when the decision was made about you," she explained.

"So, I kind of owe him my life?" Amelia asked.

"In a way, but I wouldn't mention it," she hinted. "We'll be on the first plane, with the other members of the Royal family," she said proudly.

Michelle ushered her children to their grandmother, who grabbed their hands and led them up the steps, while she and her sister followed.

"Where's Robert?" Amelia asked.

"Oh, he's already here. He lives for the Celebrations. They're a lot more fun for men than they are for women. And he was giving me hell about being an hour early yesterday," she laughed.

"Why is he so excited?" Amelia asked.

"You'll find out," Michelle answered with a wink.

They all sat together. Michelle and her children with Amelia and their mother. In the first plane, she counted maybe eight people total, leaving the cabin spacious. It was a private jet, another something new for Amelia.

The flight was a little less than an hour, touching down around 10:00 in the middle of nowhere, from what she could tell. Red dirt and a few shrubs or trees dotted the nearly barren landscape. The only truly defining characteristic of the flat expanse was a large mound in the distance.

"Where *are* we?" Amelia wondered aloud standing at the opening of the plane.

"Uluru." The deep male voice behind her said as she was stepping down the short flight of stairs. She turned as her feet hit the dirt to see Ambrose standing behind her.

"Amelia, it's so nice to finally meet you all grown up. You look just like your mother and sister," he said with a wide grin. "I'm Ambrose, your grandfather for all considerations. We can leave out all the greats. Makes me feel old," he said extending his hand.

She took it with a firm grasp and a single shake. "It's great to meet you too. So, where are we again?"

He smiled, "Uluru, or you may know it as Ayers Rock."

"Oh, ok. It looks so much smaller than the pictures," she said.

"It's much bigger in person," he said turning and walking out in front of the crowd. Which if she wasn't mistaken had grown.

She inched over to Michelle. "There are a lot more people than there were before," she whispered.

"The group earlier was just a part of the Colony. We don't all live in Perth. Garkain come from all over Australia," she smiled.

Ambrose's voice shouted above the crowd. "Let's get going!" he said as he started walking out into the middle of nowhere. One by one, the group filed in behind him. She and Michelle finding their place in line, while her children stayed close to their grandmother.

"It's a bit of a walk. But trust me, we'll have time to rest once we get there," Michelle said.

After about an hour, Amelia's feet were beginning to rub blisters in the new hiking boots her mother had bought for her. She wished she had chosen her old pair of comfortable sneakers instead. She had no idea where they were going, but she prayed they got there soon.

"Almost there," Michelle whispered, reading her mind.

"Thank goodness, my feet are killing me!"

"Believe me, this is my least favorite part too."

As promised, the group began to slow, then stopped altogether. Looking ahead, she could see a large copse of trees ahead and that was about it. They truly were in the middle of nowhere.

A few minutes later and they were moving again. She also noticed that Ayer's Rock was now much closer, and larger. The slow shuffling of the group continued forward as Amelia and Michelle shuffled along with them.

She noticed Ambrose standing to the side, holding up a large iron door. As she neared the front of the group, she saw that those in front were getting shorter somehow, then realized, they were going down into the ground.

The door was between several trees, hidden from the usual passerby, and camouflaged to blend in perfectly with the dirt around it. She hesitated at the first step down, looking at Ambrose. "Welcome to the Colony, Amelia," he said.

Michelle grabbed her hand as they took the steps down together. Her mother's influence must be wearing off, as she was starting to feel the anxiety edging in again. It also didn't help that she disliked confined spaces to begin with.

The tunnel was brightly lit with bulbs every so often which helped. At least she wasn't walking into a dark hole, she thought with relief. There must be a generator somewhere.

They walked for another thirty minutes or so before the conversations gradually began to fill the silence around them. She could also tell they were beginning to climb slightly, as her legs were starting to burn.

A strange sound from further down the corridor caught her attention, a haunting noise that was also beautiful and melodic. "What's that?" she asked Michelle.

"That is a didgeridoo, and a call to the Celebration!" she smiled at Amelia.

All at once, the tunnel opened wider. The group climbed a steep grade and entered into a vacuous and overwhelming space. The walls were solid rock. The only lighting came from the bulbs and lamps that ran along extension cords on the ground. Small white tents lined the outer perimeter of the circular space.

Amelia was hit with a sudden case of déjà vu. As she looked around, she realized, they were inside the giant rock. Paintings covered the walls as she looked all around, and from somewhere she heard the sound of running water.

Parched from the trek, she made her way over to the well at the side of the cavern, taking her place in line for a cup of water. The cool liquid was like heaven to her parched lips and mouth.

From inside, Ambrose's voice sounded much louder now, bouncing from the walls. "A call to order, everyone. Everyone!"

"That means we all go and sit," Michelle explained. She noticed that her children were still with their grandmother, which meant that Michelle must have been asked to stick close to Amelia through the first day at least. To help her acclimate and answer questions. Something Amelia realized she was grateful for.

They joined the circle of others. Her mother and Ambrose the only two standing. Michelle's children came quickly to sit with them as Ambrose began to address the large crowd.

"Our Corroboree Celebration will commence shortly. But first . . ." He trailed off letting Phoebe have the floor and stepping aside.

Her voice was crisp against the walls as she addressed them all. "As you all know, twenty-five years ago, we made a bargain. Twenty-five years ago, I let my daughter go," she spoke to the crowd with emotion. "She has now returned home. Amelia, will you please join me?" she said, extending her hand in Amelia's direction.

Hesitantly, Amelia stood and picked her way through the crowded floor of people, taking her place at her mother's side. More than a little peeved she wasn't let in on the decision to bring her up on stage to be shown off.

"I implore you to make her feel welcome. Regardless of her bloodline, regardless of everything, she is a part of the Colony, she is family, and she is *my* daughter," her mother said with more than a hint of protectiveness and authority in her last statement.

"This week, she will make the choice to Unbind, or not. It is *her* choice. I've explained some of our customs, but some will come as a shock. Please answer any questions she has honestly and make her feel like the family she is."

Her mother gave her a gentle nudge to re-take her seat. She was grateful to be spared having to make a speech at least.

"Enjoy, be merry, and have fun!" Ambrose shouted, taking over the floor, as the haunting sound of the didgeridoos and drums filled the hall again. Members of the group all sprang to their feet as the music created a lively and exuberant atmosphere.

CURIOUSER AND CURIOUSER

"Let's go!" Michelle said as the tribal music reverberated around them, pulling Amelia to her feet. Everyone in the cave was moving in frenzied excitement. The children had run off to join a younger group playing happily in the corner, while the adults busied themselves with the Celebration.

The atmosphere was buoyant with inhibition and glee. Everyone was having a fantastic time, unhinged in their movements and activities. Amelia watched in awe as some of the Garkain performed fantastic feats, scaling up the wall and flipping over and back to the ground. Others gravitated toward the tents along the outer wall in pairs.

For nearly an hour, the celebration and music raged around them until finally, it began to calm, the fervor dying down, and a more subdued tone replaced the upbeat music. She glimpsed her mother coming toward her, Ambrose by her side. Both smiling. It was a new and nice look for them, Amelia thought.

"Are you enjoying yourself so far?" her mother asked.

"It's all so overwhelming. I had no idea!" Amelia said, catching her breath.

"It's a fantastic time for us, to let loose and be ourselves, without human eyes. This is the one time we can be truly free!" Ambrose excitedly told her. "Enjoy yourself, explore. Tonight, is a night for fun." He patted her on the shoulder, moving on and leaving her with her mother.

"Have you had a chance to meet anyone? Talk to anyone?" her mother asked.

"No, not yet. I'm still taking everything in honestly." Amelia said.

"Let me know if you need anything or have any questions."

Amelia thought for a second. "Bathroom?" Her mother laughed out loud. There was a lightness to everyone's spirit here, which was refreshing. This was the first time she'd seen her mother so unguarded and spirited. Unfiltered in a way. It was nice to see her let down her guard and be less formal.

"This way," she said waving an arm for Amelia to follow her. Around a small curve, there was a crevice cut into the wall. It wasn't private or sanitary, mostly a hole in the ground, but with a seat at least.

"Thanks, I think," Amelia said.

Her mother excused herself back to the party leaving Amelia to herself.

The members of the Colony continued the boisterous dancing on and on into the night as she stood off to the side observing. Although she couldn't see the sun or the stars, she felt it was growing later.

"There you are!" Michelle's voice broke through the noise. "I thought I lost you."

"Where would I go?" Amelia laughed.

"True! Hey, I know you're getting tired. Mere humans like us can't keep up with these Garkain raves. Follow me. I got us a tent. One that hasn't been used," she said with a grin. "I thought you might want a quieter place. We'll just have to share with the younger group."

Amelia followed her through the still raucous gathering taking place in the main cavern. In the furthest corner was a larger tent, away from the others, a bit more secluded in an alcove. Opening the flap, she saw rows of sleeping teens and several children including Michelle's.

"Our cots are over here," she said whispering and motioning to the canvas wall up against the rock. Their bags were stowed underneath as well. Amelia sat, immediately stripping off her boots and socks, letting her tired feet breathe.

"How can they sleep?" Amelia pointed to the passed-out group on the other cots, or in sleeping bags on the floor. "Kids can sleep through anything," she shrugged. "Soon enough it'll quiet down. Or at least the music will."

Michelle took off her shoes as well, and then to Amelia's surprise undressed completely in front of her, changing into her nightclothes.

"Oh my God, Michelle!" Amelia said, covering her eyes.

"Modesty isn't a thing around here, and we're both women. You'll see plenty of naked butts by the time the weekend's over too," she chuckled.

Amelia stripped of her jeans, leaving on her underwear and quickly pulling on her jogging pants. She decided to take her bra off but left her shirt on. She didn't care about how modest everyone else wasn't, it was still a thing for her.

The temperature had been warm all day and into the afternoon, with so many moving bodies. But now that it was getting later, the temperature had started to fall inside the rock. And there were blankets on each of the beds, which told her it may get colder as the night went on.

The cots were comfortable, not exactly hotel and penthouse suite kind of comfortable, but better than the sleeping bags on the ground, she imagined. As Michelle had promised, the noises around them grew quieter and quieter. The music ended, and the conversations dulled in volume. But now, above everything, she could hear other sounds. Intimate sounds coming from all around.

"Michelle," she whispered.

"Hmmm?"

"Is that? Are they?" Amelia asked in shock.

"Yup. Mating season," she laughed quietly. "I'll tell you more about it in the morning."

Amelia laid there, tossing and turning. She was so tired, but the noises were beyond distracting. She tried to block out the private noises that filled her ears with the pillow, but it did little to help. Some of the sounds were loud too. Finally, like a child, she couldn't help but giggle for a solid minute. At least they were having fun, she thought.

At some point she drifted off, her tired mind quieting, and shutting down. Michelle actually had to wake her up in the morning. "Hey sleepyhead, you don't want to miss breakfast," she said with a gentle nudge.

Amelia hadn't eaten since yesterday, she realized. And she was starving! The mere mention of food made her stomach growl in anticipation.

She carefully put her bra back on and her shoes, not bothering to change from her jogging pants.

As she had guessed, it did get cold during the night. Just before she drifted off, she had pulled the blanket over her, which she was grateful for. It was still cold, as she shivered a bit, coming out from under it.

A long table had been set up, with an electric cooktop behind. A man stood at the grill top, flipping pancakes and scrambling eggs, stirring around potatoes. It looked delicious. Amelia was starving by the time they made it into the line. This was by far the nicest camping experience she'd ever had.

She followed behind Michelle grabbing her plate and choosing quite a bit from the buffet-style layout. Yesterday there was no lunch or dinner. And if that were the case today, she wanted to stuff herself while she had the chance.

She followed Michelle back to their tent with their plates, sitting on their bunks. "So, what was all that last night?" Amelia said between bites, trying not to laugh.

Michelle smiled. "I told you, that's why Robert was an hour early to get on the plane! The Celebrations are when we expand our bloodline."

"Expand the bloodline, as in mating rituals?" Amelia gawked.

"It's not as antiquated as it sounds. So, male Garkain can produce offspring, but female Garkain can't conceive. So, at the age of twenty, all eligible females engage in mating rituals. Once they produce two healthy children, they can Unbind. This ensures that the bloodline continues."

"Can't you just turn other people into Garkain?" Amelia asked.

"No, it's not that simple. The trait to become Garkain is genetic. It runs in the bloodline. We're careful about the process of selection too. One of the reasons the colonization in 1788 was so significant is that the Garkain gene pool was shrinking. Newly settled females were selected for mating and the bloodline became more diverse over time."

"It sounds so contrived. What about love or marriage?" Amelia asked.

"We don't believe in monogamy per se. But there are life mates that you see from time to time. The only love story I've ever heard of is our mothers, which isn't a great example. Other than your being here, of course," Michelle said sheepishly. "The thing is, Garkain aren't bound by time, and an eternity to spend with just one person, without getting tired of them is rare. Even for a human life span, it's rare," Michelle said with a shrug.

"That explains why there are so many different cultures and ethnicities within the Colony then," Amelia said.

"That would be correct. When Australia became more than just a land of exile, more people moved here, commerce and industry were established. We became more and more diverse with each generation. There's no discrimination here. We're all family," Michelle said smiling.

"So, Robert has to Unbind with you and me. But what about everyone else? Non-royals?"

"For both men and women, no later than twenty-five. That's why women begin trying to conceive at twenty. It gives them several years to try. If they don't produce offspring within that time, they're considered servants, the lowest in stature. That one, I don't agree with. Because we, you and I, are exempt from that rule.

"I *wanted* to have children. I wasn't required to. It's important to keep the bloodline growing, but I don't agree that there should be a punishment for things beyond your control. Some men, like Trevor, don't have the ability to produce children, which is why he's our mother's valet," she said.

"Sounds like a kind of caste system. And I agree it's unfair," Amelia said.

"It's a holdover from times long ago. Our mother and Ambrose have been trying to change it for some time. But there's only so much they can do. The council is made up of the eldest of the Garkain. Seven in total, with two royal advocates. Our mother and Ambrose are those two. Someday it could be one of us."

"So, what's on the agenda for today? *Is* there an agenda to this thing?" Amelia asked.

"No, not really. They do the same things each time, but there's no set schedule. Except for the Unbinding ritual, that will be the day before we leave. So, three days from now. Then we have the story of our colonization, which I can tell you, but Ambrose is a better storyteller than I am.

"But the mating will go on for the entire time. It seems strange, but it's consensual, and from my experience, enjoyable," she raised her eyebrows and smirked, making Amelia laugh.

Throughout the day she came to know some of the others in the Colony. Some human, some Garkain. Everyone was friendly and welcoming. Although she didn't feel quite comfortable asking a lot of questions yet, she mostly observed and carried on polite and light topics of conversation. She answered a lot of questions about Texas and the States, but she did feel like part of the family for sure.

That night, there was dinner thankfully. She and Michelle ate in their tents again along with the children. They were kind of like the chaperones of the Celebration for now, which Amelia didn't mind at all.

She did find it easier to sleep the second night. The sounds easier to block out, and not quite as shocking. The next morning over breakfast they were all told to assemble in the main chamber. And she finally figured out why Michelle kept pulling her into the tent for each meal. She watched as human after human were set in chairs.

"What are they doing?"

"Donating breakfast," Michelle explained. "It's perfectly safe. We have several phlebotomists within the

Colony. All licensed. Watch, I'll donate this morning," she said, standing and excusing one of the others from their seat.

Amelia watched as a woman carefully inserted a catheter and a line into the crook of Michelle's arm. A bag hung on the side of the chair, slowly filling with her blood. Once she was done, she was unhooked, given a band-aid, and came back to join her sister.

"Just like giving blood at a blood bank. Humans have to eat real food, but Garkain need to the good stuff, straight from the vein," Michelle joked, finishing her breakfast.

"You make it sound so normal . . ."

"You'll have to remember, I've been coming to the Celebrations for over ten years. This is our culture. Our way of life. This is who we are. For you, I'm sure it's a shock. For me, it is completely normal. I didn't mean to upset you, or offend you," Michelle said with a worried tone.

"No, you didn't. I just. I need to get used to my new life that's all. As you said, you've had over a decade to experience all of this. I'm seeing it all for the first time. I'm doing my best to understand it all, but it's a lot to take in all at once."

"I completely understand, and we'll eat in the tent again from now on. It's just that Ambrose is about to tell the story this morning, so we all had to come see his performance," she smiled, taking Amelia's plate and carrying it back to the serving table for her.

She came back and sat cross-legged next to Amelia, waving for her kids to come and sit with them. They waited patiently until Ambrose came out from his tent, taking the middle of the room as his stage.

A SPECIAL GIRL?

The entire room became so deathly silent, you could hear people breathing. An anticipatory pall hung over the room as Ambrose waited for his moment to begin.

"When my mother first came to this country it was called New Holland," he began. "She was a prisoner from England, one of the first shipped here in 1788, just after this great land became a dumping ground for the less desirable. She was the first of our bloodline to come to this country, followed soon after by others who sought sanctuary, anonymity, and safety. I was born two years later in 1790. She may have been the first of our bloodline to come to this land, but not the last.

"This is the story of our beginning, the history of our Colony, which I have the great pleasure of passing on," he paused, pacing for dramatic effect.

"The land here is harsh, very little water, and only the toughest survive. But it was safe for our kind. In Europe, the Venandi sought to find and eradicate us from the Earth. And so, along with my mother, others of our kind chose to call New Holland home. Here we were safe from the hunters.

"The indigenous people of this land welcomed us and in return, we welcomed them, accepting their culture, their ways, and their customs. We became a family and formed the Colony, the Council, and the rules for our society.

"Garkain blood flows through our veins. But we are all descended from the first Garkain immortal. Some legends say that we were created at the same time as humans, other cultures claim to be responsible for our creation. The truth is, that the story has been lost to time. However, stories of our kind do exist in each and every culture around the world. As for me, I can only tell you how we, the Uluru Colony were created.

"The Unbinding ritual is still performed as it was eons ago, passed down from generation to generation. And in two days, some of you will join the Colony, our family, for eternity."

Ambrose finished with a bow, and the roaring applause of his crowd.

"What exactly is the ritual?" Amelia asked. "No one's told me yet."

Michelle sighed. "It's not that complicated. But it's also not fun, from what I've heard, and seen. The Garkain breakfast you saw me give this morning is part of it. Only you'll drink the blood of our mother, a direct bloodline link first," she paused, thinking.

"I'm guessing the next part is the bad part," Amelia said.

"Well, you kind of have to die," she said with a grimace.

"Wait, what do you mean, I have to die!" Amelia shouted a little too loudly.

Michelle put her finger to her lips, imploring Amelia to lower her voice. She stood and waved her sister toward the tent, so they could talk in a more secluded place.

"Hey, you two, I was wondering where you went, you left in such a hurry," Their mother caught them, following them inside the tent and lowering her voice. "I heard you two talking. We all did," she said with obvious disappointment.

"She asked about the ritual, and I was trying to explain it as gently as I could," Michelle tried to assure her. "Look, I've seen it happen hundreds of times, and it's not that bad," she said to Amelia, who had started to hyperventilate.

"Shhh, darling calm down. Calm down. Just breathe with me. Breathe with me," her mother said clasping her hands around Amelia's, breathing slowly, until both of their patterns matched, slow and steady.

"Yes, you will have to Unbind from your mortality, which means you'll have to give it up first. When you awaken, you'll be one of us, Garkain. Everyone dies once in this life. You just have to do it once when you're young, then you have forever to live."

Amelia thought as her mother spoke. The way she explained it, it made a strange kind of sense. She had a way of explaining things that were crazy, making them sound nearly normal. Acceptable.

All things died eventually, but if she chose to die now, she would come back, and live for hundreds or even thousands of years. It still didn't make the prospect of dying any less scary.

"How does it happen?" Amelia asked fearfully.

"You saw Michelle this morning. We'll do the same for you. Once you take my blood, you will be drained of all your human blood. My Garkain blood inside you will start to seep into your heart, restarting it. When you awaken, you'll take more and more human blood until you're fully back on your feet. I've already given several liters over these few days for the three of you."

"I'm scared," Amelia admitted, not at all adjusting to the biggest piece of the puzzle being pushed into place.

"I know my darling. And you can still change your mind. We wouldn't force you to do anything you didn't want to."

"Does it hurt?" Amelia asked her mother, tears threatening her eyes.

"Not at all. At first, you'll feel drowsy, and then you'll fall asleep. We'll be there the whole time," her mother assured her, glancing between her daughters.

"Take the day today to think about it. This time, we're doing things a little differently. We have more that will undergo the ritual this Celebration, so we'll be starting tomorrow. You can watch then and decide," her mother said.

Amelia nodded, thinking. "Okay, okay. That I can do."

"I'll leave you two to talk. And your children are driving me crazy," she said to Michelle.

"You always say that! And you were the one who offered to watch them while I stayed with Amelia," Michelle shot back.

So she was right, Michelle *had* been assigned to her. She wondered if she was also tasked with talking her into Unbinding.

As their mother excused herself, leaving the two of them alone again. Amelia decided to be upfront with her sister.

"Are you supposed to talk me into the ritual, into Unbinding?"

Michelle looked shocked for a moment, and then a bit saddened. "They did ask me to try and persuade you. But I'm trying to help you lean that way because now that I have a sister, I don't want to lose you," she said.

Amelia believed her. Could feel her honesty, and her guilt. "I don't like being misled," Amelia said with conviction, the slightest bit of betrayal creeping into her heart.

"I can't blame you for being pissed. But just know that what I said about not wanting to lose you is true. And I want you to ask some other Garkain. About their experience, about why they chose to Unbind, and if it was worth it. I'm on your side. I want you to make the choice that you want to make. Let me introduce you to a couple of my friends. It's been just me and you this whole time anyway. Hear about it from someone outside the immediate family, okay? Someone unbiased," she said.

Michelle peeked out of the tent and within minutes two other girls were inside with them.

"Amelia, this is Claire and Marilyn. Guys, this is my sister Amelia," Michelle introduced them.

"The famous Amelia," Claire said. "We finally meet."

"Why does everyone say that, acting like I'm something so special?"

"Because you are. Larougo and Garkain? You're *literally* the first of your kind," Marilyn jumped in.

"Enough guys, she's worried about the Unbinding. And I wanted to give her the chance to ask someone besides me and my mother. Someone who's been through the process before. And as two of the most viscously honest people I know, I thought you could tell her. Give her the straight scoop."

"Kind of freaking out about the whole having to die thing. You know, not something you usually volunteer to do," Amelia said.

"Believe me, I was the same way. But it's not that bad honestly. I've been Unbound for only about six years now, but I remember going through the ritual clearly. I think the worst part is having to choke down the blood at first. After you're Unbound you can't get enough. But at first, it's pretty gross," Marilyn said with a face.

"But after that it's amazing. The strength, the speed, the gift, not to mention you never have to die again!" Claire jumped in.

"And no, it doesn't hurt. It feels like you're falling asleep and then you wake up starving. Getting used to all the perks is a process, and you'll have someone like a mentor to help you get used to feeding, and using the gift, how to blend in, things like that," Marilyn continued.

"And how long have you been Unbound?" Amelia asked Claire.

"Seventy-two years, and still looking good, yet another perk," she smiled as she twirled.

"What are the downsides? There has to be some bad to go with the good," Amelia fished.

Claire sighed, thinking. "Having to blend in, to take time in the sun, to let your skin protect itself. Not being able to enjoy your favorite foods anymore, because they don't taste the same. And having to constantly keep reinventing yourself. Going dark for a decade or so, living off the grid so people don't start getting suspicious because you don't age," Claire explained.

Amelia tried to keep track of all the information that was flying by her so fast. Of course, she'd expected some downsides. But the benefits, so far, seemed to outweigh the cons. At least she was attempting to see it that way.

"There's one thing though that's tough for almost everyone, but probably tougher for you. Cutting ties with your previous life. Friends, family, *boyfriend* if you have one. Anyone that would know you too well not to notice things," Marilyn said. "We're all from the Colony, so we never needed to worry about that, but you would. If you did Unbind."

"I have a foster family. I was adopted, but I was never that close with them. Still not that close with them honestly. Really the only thing about my life back home I might miss is my job, and some of the people I work with," Amelia admitted.

"Then you'll do fine. I really do hope you decide to join us tomorrow. You could move to Australia. We could hang out. It would be super cool and awesome!" Marilyn said.

"Okay guys, you're getting a little too overworked. Let's get out of here and walk around for a bit. It's getting close to dinner anyway," Michelle offered, sensing that Amelia had had about enough conversation for one afternoon.

Marilyn and Claire suddenly spun their heads toward the flap of the tent. Amelia noticed that the sounds of conversation had died down a bit outside as well. The two girls jumped to their feet and flew out of the tent with lightning speed, leaving Amelia and Michelle alone.

A general unease had settled among the room outside.

"What's going on?" Amelia asked.

"I don't know," Michelle said as they both stood and cautiously walked out into the open. A quiet whispering chatter filled the room. Low and with a sense of something wrong. Amelia was on edge, and she could tell Michelle was too.

Their mother came running to them, along with Michelle's children.

"What's going on?" Michelle asked. Their mother was definitely on guard, and edgy, just as they all were.

"I don't know. Someone is banging on the door to the outside. Ambrose is going through the tunnels now." Their mother moved to stand in front of them, as they all waited.

The entire group stood together, a solid wall of Garkain and human, while the four of them stayed near the tent behind them, waiting.

Over the silence, Ambrose's voice loudly sounded, bouncing off the rock walls. "Amelia!"

Amelia looked from Michelle to her mother, seeing confusion cross both of their faces. The crowd in front of them parted. Ambrose and another man stood at the opening to the tunnel.

"Anatole," her mother said softly. "The leader of Lachlean's pack."

"Larougo?" Amelia whispered.

Her mother simply nodded as she took her daughter's hand and led her through the middle of the crowd to meet the son of the man who had killed her father.

A DANGEROUS GIRL?

Anatole, the Larougo leader, waited patiently as both Amelia and her mother approached. She squeezed her mothers' hand, receiving a gentle reassuring squeeze in return.

"So, this is Lachlean's girl?" he said coldly, looking her up and down. She could feel her mother trying to control her anger beside her.

"I don't see much of him in her, but then again, Lachlean didn't have the strongest genes. Perhaps she won't have any Larougo traits at all. Then again, I could be wrong," he said.

Her mother was maintaining herself, trying her hardest to show no emotion as Amelia shook her hand free of her tightening grip.

Amelia bravely stepped forward. "Any words you would like to address to me?" she asked, staring boldly into the young face of the Larougo leader, whose true age showed in the tiredness of his eyes.

"Maybe there is a bit of him in you after all," he smiled. "Do you plan to Unbind? Have you made your choice?" he addressed her in a slightly less aggressive and more curious way.

"I have," Amelia said loud and clearly. She'd been steadily leaning toward that choice anyhow, but now she was resolved. A hushed few words passed through the group behind her. Ambrose grinned.

"And what do you know of your other bloodline, your father's bloodline? What have you been told?" Anatole asked, leaning in toward her.

"Very little. Only that my mother loved him very much. And that because of me, he lost his life," Amelia said, meeting his stare, defiant and challenging. With the whole Colony standing behind her she felt brave, protected, and emboldened.

"You know your mother's side of the story, clearly," he huffed.

"I'd like you to come with me," he said, then turned to Ambrose. "Just for the night, one night. She's been introduced to your culture, and I think it would be prudent for her to know a bit about the Larougo way of life and culture. Say she does share the traits of both our bloodlines, she should understand our ways as well. Our rules."

"It would be her choice," Ambrose said in a flat tone. "But I agree that she should have the opportunity to know more about her father's pack."

She turned and looked to her mother, whose eyes told her to make her own choice. She looked to Ambrose whose face betrayed no emotion at all. She wished she had some input to help her make a choice.

"I don't know you, so I can't trust you. I won't go with you alone," Amelia decided. "But I will go with my sister," she said.

Footsteps sounded behind her as Michelle stepped forward and stood by her sister. "It would be my pleasure," she said.

The two of them stood side by side, as Anatole thought for a moment, looking at them with interest. "You're both human."

"We are," Michelle answered for them both.

"I'll agree to it," Anatole said. "The sun has just gone down, and we have only eight or so hours together. If you're ready, we can go now. If not, please quickly grab what you need, and we'll be on the way."

"We're ready," Amelia spoke for them this time.

"Wonderful! Ambrose, if you'll show us out, we will return at sunrise," Anatole and Ambrose bowed to one another, showing each other a strained respect.

Ambrose leaned in to whisper something to Michelle, too low for Amelia to hear. She nodded and they were off, walking back down the long lighted corridor together, Ambrose following up behind the group.

As soon as they were at the bottom of the steep grade, conversation loudly resumed in their absence among the members of the Colony. Gossip flowed from one to another as the sounds faded the further they walked.

The tunnel gradually began to rise again, Ambrose speaking up from behind them. "Anatole, my granddaughters are to be treated with respect and come to no harm. Am I in any way unclear?" he said with all the authority of both a leader and a grandfather.

"You have my word," Anatole said.

"That's good. I would hate for our truce to come to an end, as it almost did twenty-five years ago," Ambrose said in a way that could only be taken as a threat.

"As would I. It would be a shame indeed," Anatole let his own threat hang in the air as Ambrose inched by them, opening the door to the outside with a cold rush of air.

They climbed the few steps and were on solid ground again, met by a circle of Larougo, who abruptly stopped talking as the two women appeared.

The sisters stood still and silent, intimidated by the gathering in front of them. So many strangers, so many different looks.

"Roan, will you please introduce yourself? Ladies, my son Roan will be your guide and accompany you through the night," Anatole held out his hand waving his son from the crowd.

Her first thought was how incredibly handsome, attractive, and intriguing he was. Her next thought was, how could someone like Anatole have a son like this? She shook both thoughts from her mind, as he came closer to them.

"Ladies. It's a pleasure to meet you both. I'm guessing you," he said turning his dark eyes toward her, "are Amelia."

"How did you know?" Michelle asked.

"A sense I have. Just a hunch. I remember your father, you remind me of him, in some way I can't quite put my finger on," He said, flashing a bright smile. "Come on ladies, we'll lead the pack, so to speak. And we can talk later," he whispered to Amelia.

She didn't trust him. Not yet at least. And she doubted that Michelle did either. But for some reason, her intuition was telling her that she should. He led off, not even glancing back to make sure they were following. Amelia and Michelle had to jog to catch up, passing warily through the group.

Amelia chanced to lean in close to Michelle, whispering as quietly as she could. "What did Ambrose tell you? Before we left?"

Michelle turned her head, her breath moving Amelia's hair as she spoke. "He said to take care of you."

Amelia smiled, then grabbed her sister's hand, mouthing the words 'thank you', as they continued their hike.

"Where are we going?" Amelia asked after a while. Her blisters were making themselves known again already.

"Not much farther, our den is only a few kilos from your Colony, underground. Though probably not as nicely accommodated as yours. We're in our dingo form most of the time, during the day. We hunt and forage for a while, then sleep while it's hot. We don't need much in the way of plush amenities," he explained without the air of judgement that she expected.

"I thought werewolves, I mean lycanthropes, I'm sorry. I thought there was something to do with the moon?" Amelia dared to ask, instantly embarrassed.

"Just call us Larougo, it's so much easier to say. You read a lot, don't you?" he asked with a laugh.

"Why does everyone keep saying that?" Amelia said with frustration.

"Because you've got a little bit of that mixed with a little bit of this. It's totally Hollywood and not at all based on how things are now, although it used to be a once a month thing, now it's every day and night.

"See, most people understand the way we were, how history has made both of our kinds out to be. All species change over time, humans, plants, Garkain, and Larougo. I'll bet your people aren't exactly what you expected either," he said as he glanced at her.

"That's true," Amelia had to agree.

"And most of the literary works that feature either of our kind were based on speculation anyhow. Half-truths. It's not like we have a Twitter page where people can just go ask us questions and get real answers. And back when all the legends were turned into truth, we were in hiding. We couldn't hold a town conference and explain our side of things," he laughed again. Not in a mean way, more amused than mocking.

"So what's the real story?" Amelia probed.

"What's the real story with you? I'm betting you don't know either. Our history is kind of the same way. From what I've pieced together, various versions of Garkain and

Larougo exist in every culture from every time, from all around the world.

"Some version of our people date back thousands of years B.C. No one truly knows. All we know is that, like you, the gene travels through offspring, parent to child. It's a dominant gene. Which is why we're so curious about you in particular," he said.

"Do you have a degree in this or something?" Michelle snarked at him. He was a bit haughty with the over-explaining.

"Actually, I have two, one in Anthropology, and one in Genetics. We get cell phone signal out here sometimes. I got my degrees online," he quipped back.

Amelia wanted to smile but tried to keep a straight face. "So, I ask again. Why am I of such interest? It's like both Garkain and Larougo are worried about me in particular because I have two separate bloodlines. Why is that?" Amelia asked.

"For one, once you decide to Unbind, whichever gene is most dominant will dictate which attributes you're most likely to display. Either Garkain or Larougo. The other possibility is that you could have both in equal parts. Like a child born to parents of differing ethnicities. Most likely some of the more dominant traits would be passed down, such as dark eyes, or brown hair.

"Other times, one of the recessive genes peeks through or mingles with the dominant gene. The same pair of parents could have another child with the hazel eyes of her father, and lighter complexion than that of her brother. From a genetics standpoint, it's a roll of the dice."

He explained it patiently, and in a way that Amelia could understand. For them, it was curiosity more than anything. Or at least that's what she hoped.

"What if I have both? What would that mean for me? What if I'm mostly Larougo?" Amelia asked hesitantly.

Roan sighed. "If you have both traits, equally. It would mean that your mother and father created something completely new, or at least unlike anyone we've heard of. And we don't yet know what that would mean. Our Larougo side is triggered very simply. All we have to do is die at the hands of a family member. My father killed me. So, when you Unbind from your mortal self, your mother would be the one to drain you of your blood, if I'm understanding your ritual correctly," he said in a studious almost detached, and academic way.

Michelle and Amelia both nodded.

"Right, so, it *should* trigger both genes. It just depends on which one is stronger. If it does happen to be the Larougo gene, you'll also be immortal, but you'll be human only at night. Which is kind of difficult. We don't have much of a social life outside of the pack. It also means that you could develop glands under the root of your nail beds, in both forms, human and dingo. All of this is purely hypothetical mind you. We truly won't know more until you Unbind."

A mound rising from the landscape slowly came closer as the pack behind them became more energetic. Amelia guessed that this was their den.

One by one they crawled through the hole in the mound down and down until, to her relief, it began to open into a large and darkly lit cavern, similar to, but not nearly as big as the Garkain space.

There were dozens of corridors off the main living area, going who knew where. There were no tents or fancy cots. There were no sleeping arrangements that she could see at all as she looked around. Rooms must be down the tunnel offshoots from the main cavern, Amelia thought. Dozens of indentions dotted the ground, a steady dipping like the oversized surface of a golf ball.

"Welcome to the den," Roan said as they entered.

"Yes, welcome. I trust Roan has been an informative and polite guide thus far?" Anatole asked, coming to stand in front of the small group. The other Larougo had either gone down one of the various tunnels or busied themselves on the ground with one thing or another. Trying to eavesdrop and appear unconcerned at the same time.

"Very and thank you. I have to ask. Why did you want me to come tonight?" she asked Anatole.

"To learn about your other culture, your other bloodline as I said. Would you mind if we spoke in private for a moment?" he asked Amelia.

She looked to her sister then nodded, following him down one of the short corridors into a slightly brighter room, leaving Michelle and Roan to themselves.

The room was furnished, to her surprise. A small bed, a bookshelf, and a pair of chairs with a desk helped to give the space a homier feel. She assumed that this would be Anatole's room, and much nicer than any of the others.

"Would you like to sit?" he asked, pulling out the chair from behind the desk, sitting and offering the other to

Amelia. Tired from the walk, she was more than happy to take him up on the offer. He waited for her to take a seat before he began.

"I'd like you to relax. You're nervous, I can tell. But I don't mean to harm you. The way that Roan explained everything. Does it make sense?" he asked, his attitude much improved. Bordering on friendly even.

"I think so," she said honestly.

"In the old days, way before my time, in Europe and across other parts of the world where Garkain and Larougo occupied the same space, there was constant war. In other parts of the world there may still be groups of our kind at odds. We each have our own very strong opinions, and a very strong allegiance to our sides, as I'm sure you can tell.

"When both our kinds were nearly hunted to extinction, our two groups, led by my late father and Ambrose's mother, made a pact. To join forces, to put whatever centuries-old rivalry we'd been entangled in aside. Both groups came to New Holland together. Slowly over time, making a home here in secret.

"Once here, we went our separate ways, and the truce remains unbroken. By working together and putting aside our differences, respecting each other's space, and cultures, we were able to survive. To flourish over time," he paused letting Amelia take all of this in, to process.

"What I'm about to propose, I've already discussed with Ambrose. And he's agreeable if you are. Your great-grandfather is very big on free will. He said that your choice in all things must be respected. And I agree. But what I'm about to propose will depend on what happens once you

Unbind." He paused again, waiting for her to say something if she wanted.

When she didn't speak, he continued. "If you are truly both Larougo and Garkain, if you have both traits, it would be a way for us to co-exist in an even deeper way. A new beginning. That's why I'm asking you now to consider marrying my son."

A BOLD PROPOSAL

Amelia sat stunned. Stuck silent and utterly unable to form words. Did she hear that right? Was she asleep, all of this a dream? Surely, he was joking, but the somber and resolute face he wore now, told her he wasn't.

"You're serious?" she asked.

"I am. Garkain don't believe in marriage, they don't believe in monogamy, but we do. Although we call it a joining instead of marriage. Larougo aren't bound by the reproductive constraints that Garkain are either. You may be able to have children. Children, who would hopefully share the same unique genetics you do," he said.

"If that's the case, then why was I sent away when I was born? Why did you kill my father? If this is what you wanted all along, why would you do all of that?" she yelled, angry at the man in front of her.

Decades of struggling to fit in anywhere flashed through her memory. The uncertainty of flitting between homes until she found a family willing to take a chance on poor orphaned Amelia. Her constant longing for answers, and a desperate search for her biological family never should have happened. She felt cheated. Hurt, and angry.

"I can tell you that my father, not me, was the one who led our pack at that time. A mistake was made. A mistake we tried to rectify. We searched for you, Amelia. Both Ambrose and I did. We began searching when you would have been about six.

"But until you took the DNA test, we had no way of finding you. I am sorry about what happened then. But it wasn't me, it wasn't my decision. And to be honest, the decision he made wasn't highly favored. My father acted independently, without approval. And for that he paid the same price as your father," he said leaning over the small desk, his elbows nearly taking up the entire top.

Amelia wanted to cry. Her whole life could have been different, should have been different. Her emotions were running wild inside. Resentment and sorrow mixed with outright sadness as she thought again of the hard twenty-five years she'd lived.

"I need time to think. You don't understand. Up until a few days ago, I was an orphan, with an adopted family that didn't really like me. Then I come here, all the way to Australia, to finally meet my mother, who happens to be Garkain, who had me with a lycanthrope, sorry, Larougo, and now you want me to get married and have babies? Am I summing that up pretty well?" she couldn't stop the words now as they flew out of her mouth.

"In a word, yes," Anatole replied.

"You're crazy!" she said pointing at the man sitting across from her as he visibly flinched. "This is all crazy. I think I'm going to pass out," she said, trying to slow her breathing.

"Roan, water, now!" he yelled through the tunnel, standing up and coming to kneel by her.

A few seconds later, a cup of water was given to her, as she drank it down in one gulp. Anatole stayed with her, actually proving he could be nice when he wanted something. She still didn't trust him though.

"I know this is a huge thing to ask. A huge commitment," Anatole said.

"You think?" Amelia shot back, glaring at him,

"But you could be the beginning of something new, both of you. If what happens when you Unbind is what we hope, it would mean that you would be mostly Garkain. Able to stay in human form during the day, or even control the ability to transform. You would share both traits of our bloodlines. We're not sure about anything at this point. But the possibility is there.

"It would mean that your descendants could forever put an end to the possibility of another clash between our kinds. Eventually, through time, we would live in harmony, as one Colony. Can you promise me this for now? That you will think about it seriously? That you will give it the sincere consideration it deserves? Weigh the pros and cons, see the everlasting benefit to this?" Anatole pleaded with her.

She finally looked up at him again. Her initial reaction had passed, as she began to think more logically. More analytically.

"What would be the benefit for my people?" she asked, realizing that her first allegiance was to the Colony, the Garkain. Her people, not theirs.

"We think if Roan is correct. Your progeny, your descendants would be immune to the Larougo madness that the venom in our claws can cause. But there are so many benefits. A new beginning, a chance to completely change the way things are done, to change for the better, to move into a new way of living and thinking. I only want you to consider it," He said in a way that signaled he was done trying to persuade her. The choice was now in her hands.

"I will consider it, as long as you respect my right to say no," she declared.

"I will respect your free will. You have my word," he said with what Amelia felt was true sincerity. "And thank you."

"You're welcome."

"Now that we've gotten the serious stuff out of the way, let's go back to the main den, so you can observe how we live. And give you a minute to collect your thoughts."

They stood together and made their way back to the main room, finding Michelle and Roan waiting anxiously. She tried not to look at him, tried not to make eye contact. Tried not to think about how he already knew what was going on. Michelle nudged her out of her thoughts.

"How did it go?"

"We'll talk later. Alone."

Michelle nodded, as Amelia couldn't help but glance in Roan's direction. At least he was attractive, she thought. She needed to press the pause button. Her mind was on over-drive at the moment. What she really wanted to ask Michelle was, what the hell she and Roan had been talking about for the last hour.

There were more Larougo in the den now. Mothers with their children, men with their significant others, all keeping to themselves, but all sneaking a look at the two girls from the Colony.

She felt more like a curiosity than a person. But she remained polite. Smiling when she caught someone's stare. If she did agree to Anatole's crazy plan, Unbinding with both sets of traits, then these people would become a part of her life. Better safe than sorry and not start out on the wrong foot.

There was an undeniable difference in the way the Larougo lived. A very blatant difference in the way the two groups socialized and survived. They looked at her like a spoiled royal brat, when they had no idea the scars and pains she held inside from her past.

She felt him walk up beside her before he spoke. "We don't do a lot of partying like your people do, what you see is mostly what goes on. We're a quiet people," Roan said, reinforcing the stereotype she was afraid they already had of her. Let them think what they wanted, she thought.

"What do *you* do for fun?" Amelia asked.

"Read mostly or write. I'm a curious person. I like to read or research things. Learn new things. I like to help others with projects when I can," he told her.

He sounded like a Tinder profile. Oh crap, she thought. He took it as a personal get to know you question. Despite the chill in the den, she felt her face warm as she blushed. She turned away to hide it, only to see Michelle grinning.

"You may not know this about me, but up until four days ago, I had no idea about any of this. I'm still getting used to the idea of just having found my family after twenty-five years. So, the rest of it is a little hard to swallow at the moment.

"Whatever happens when I Unbind, this whole experience has been a roller coaster ride of surprises. Just so you know," Amelia said, alluding to the fact she knew what was going on, without addressing it publicly.

"Oh, I completely understand," Roan said smiling. "Anatole filled me in on the whole story. And your accent is a dead giveaway that you're a little new here. Just saying," he said with a chuckle.

As much as Amelia wanted to dislike him, she couldn't deny the fact that he'd been polite and respectful their entire time together. Maybe he wasn't so bad, she thought.

Generic chitchat filled the rest of their time together, as Amelia tried to stop herself from glancing at Roan's direction. She tried to divorce herself from thinking about Roan in any other way than a friend or an acquaintance, but despite her best efforts she couldn't help replaying the conversation with Anatole earlier. Imagining the future he had so boldly proposed.

"So, I wanted to ask. Larougo are only here in Australia?" Amelia asked Roan.

He shook his head. "No, just like Garkain, there are Larougo packs all over the world. We don't see each other often, but we know that they exist. My father and the other pack leaders talk from time to time. Keep in contact, but it's minimal. We're all separate, with our own leaders and laws."

"And how can it be that I'm the first Larougo and Garkain to exist?" Amelia asked.

"Just because we made peace together here, doesn't mean that all Garkain and Larougo are in a, shall we say, friendly relationship like ours. We're unique because of our circumstances. If the hysteria in England had never happened, if the Venandi had never been formed, we might not have had to form an alliance. We may have stayed in Europe. Finding our way here eventually, but not with the strong alliance we formed back then," he explained.

"What we did was come together for survival. If we hadn't banded together, we would have all been hunted to extinction."

"Then I guess all things happen for a reason," Michelle jumped in trying to put a positive spin on the story. She felt left out Amelia knew. The conversation had been mostly between her and Roan.

The hours gradually moved along and soon it would be time for her to make the long trek back to the Colony. And it wasn't long before Anatole came into the room again, standing over the three in conversation.

"It's nearly time," he said looking down. "I'm going to allow Roan to take you back to the Colony by himself if that's fine with you," he said directly to Amelia. His true intentions made the request heavy with meaning.

"Of course," she said flatly, careful to remain flippant in appearance when it came to anything Roan related. The truth was, she didn't appreciate the set-up. But she also felt more comfortable with just the three of them this time, instead of the entire pack as an escort.

"Ladies, if you'd like, we can go ahead and head out, that way we don't have to rush," Roan offered.

And more time to be alone in the dark, more time to talk, more time to get to know each other, Amelia thought snidely. Did they really think they were fooling her? She smiled at the thought.

"Fine by me," Amelia said, jumping to her feet. Michelle likewise stood, a little slower. Amelia could tell she was tired. They both were. They'd been up for nearly 24-hours straight now.

Roan led the way, the darkness still holding them tightly, with no glimmer in the Eastern sky yet. The hard ground was slightly lit by the moon, straight above them. They walked in silence for a while, until Roan dared to break the tension between them.

"I think we should talk. About what my father said to you," he said outright, which Amelia appreciated. "He came to me first about the idea, when Ambrose let us know you'd been found. I know it seems like a strange thing to agree to, but I did," he said, waiting for her to respond.

"I'm only twenty-five years old Roan. And it's not that you don't seem nice, you do. And it's not that you're not attractive, because, well you are," she said quickly, hoping the darkness would hide her blushing. "But I didn't grow up in either culture. I was raised human. With human society. American human society. It's hard for me to agree with the idea of an arranged marriage," she explained.

"I completely understand, and I'm not meaning to pressure you in any way at all, please understand that. I'm only letting you know that I'm agreeable if you are. You may not have even wanted children in your future, and I understand that too. But if it helps, I can tell you, that my instincts are usually spot-on, and I feel, I think, that you and I would make a pretty complimentary couple," he smiled, intentionally trying his best to be charming.

"I'll tell you the same as I did Anatole. I *will* think about it. I can't promise you or him any more than that. And if there are no Larougo traits that show up once I Unbind, then this whole conversation will be for nothing. So, right now, let's just mark it down as a wait and see kind of thing," she said. "Agreed?"

"Agreed," Roan said with a smirk.

Michelle had been trailing them a dozen or so feet behind, but Amelia made sure that she spoke just loudly enough so her sister could know a bit about what was going on. Michelle was smart, she knew what she was doing. Sometimes you learn *and* hear the most by appearing invisible.

At the entrance to the Colony, which at night you couldn't see at all, they stood and waited as Roan stomped loudly on the door in the ground.

"It was a pleasure meeting you, Amelia. And I'm sure we will see each other again, or at least I hope so," he said, lifting her hand and pressing his lips gently to the top.

Again, she was grateful for the darkness, as she felt the skin of her cheeks warm against the cool night air.

"You too," she said clumsily.

Thankfully a screech echoed, as the metal handle to the door was turned and the ground came alive with light, cutting their awkward goodbyes short. Ambrose stepped up and into the night, their mother at the bottom of the stairs waiting.

Amelia hurried down the few steps eager to escape the strangest blind date of her human life. Michelle said her polite goodbyes and came down after her, while Amelia waited respectfully for Ambrose to close the door before she let loose.

"What the . . . hell! You set me up!" She accused Ambrose. "You knew they were coming to get me. You knew what they were going to ask me, and you never said anything to me? Why would you do that, why would you let me get blindsided like that? You're making deals and promises for me, and I don't appreciate it!" She let her words hit where she thought they might hurt worst.

Whirling around, she turned on her mother. "Did *you* know about this?"

"Ambrose told me after you left with Anatole. I was just as upset as you are. We've had our words since you've been gone," she said glancing sidelong at Ambrose, who stood perfectly still avoiding her gaze.

"I'm tired of shit that involves *me* being left out of the loop. You two both got it?" Amelia said as she whirled around without a response.

She stomped off down the tunnel toward the main room, heading straight for her tent, then closed and tied the flap. She laid down, still fuming. Her life was slowly being decided for her, and she didn't like it one bit. Not to mention she kept having the feeling that she was being manipulated and used. Which was not a great way to get her on anyone's side. Family or not.

This backward, antiquated way of life wasn't in her. She was too independent and strong-willed to follow blindly along with something like this. Wasn't she?

She needed to think. She needed to say no, didn't she? This was crazy, wasn't it? She went over the night in her mind until she started to get sleepy. Without announcing, Michelle snuck through the side door of their tent, laying down beside her, sighing loudly.

"He is handsome," Michelle dared to strike up the conversation.

"Yeah, but could you imagine being asked to marry someone you just met? And weren't you the one who said something about getting tired of just one person for eternity?" Amelia said.

Michelle shrugged. "I could look at that for a few hundred years at least."

"You're hilarious," Amelia said with dripping sarcasm.

"Okay, it was a little bit of a surprise. A lot of a surprise." Michelle said raising her hands, as Amelia shot her a look. "But the leader of the Larougo is asking you to marry his son. Either way you look at it, that's pretty amazing.

"And for what it's worth, the time I got to spend with him, he seems like a genuinely nice guy. Maybe a little pompous at times with the knowledge, but nice," Michelle threw in.

"I just need time to think. It seems like the more I agree to things, the more I keep getting asked to do. I feel like I'm continually being nudged and persuaded."

"It's all because you're so unique. I told you that you were special."

"Yeah, well, being special feels pretty crappy right now. I don't want to talk anymore. I need to sleep. My brain is so fuzzy, you're starting to make sense," Amelia joked.

"Okay, get some rest. We'll talk more tomorrow."

"Tomorrow," Amelia agreed.

THE DECISION

She wasn't sure how long they slept, but when Amelia opened her eyes, she longed to close them again. Sleep wouldn't let her go. She wanted so badly to allow herself to fall back under.

Glancing around she noticed that Michelle wasn't in the tent. She'd already gotten up, and it wouldn't be long before someone else came looking for her.

Stuffing her tired feet back into her boots, she slowly stood, feeling a bit wobbly and certainly not fully awake yet. She prayed there was still coffee left from breakfast. Although she had no clue what time it was.

She untied the front flaps of the tent and stepped out into the great room. There was a calm about things, as if the four straight days of partying had finally worn them all out.

Either that or . . . Suddenly she remembered that her mother had said the schedule for this Celebration had changed. Both today and tomorrow there would be Unbinding rituals performed.

Spotting her mother and Ambrose amid a group in the corner she made her way to them, her brain still foggy from lack of sleep and running on empty. She tried to sort through her feelings, decide where to begin, how to start the topic of last night. But nothing was coming.

"We need to talk," she said simply as she drew herself upright, standing as tall as her tired frame would allow.

"Alright," Ambrose answered her.

"Not you," she shot back at him with a deadly serious look. "My mother and I need to talk," she said again, this time directly to her.

"Please excuse us, Ambrose," her mother said, removing herself from his side and following Amelia to a secluded corner.

"Explain," Amelia demanded.

"As soon as your tone changes, I will," her mother shot back as Amelia noticed her mother's anger directed at her for the first time. She'd never seen her angry until now. Not that it mattered to her, she was the one who had the right to be angry, not Phoebe.

"My tone? My tone is not the issue. The issue is that you and my great whatever grandfather went behind my back and offered me up as a bargaining tool. Did you at least throw in a goat and two cows?" she quipped, letting her sharp tongue do the talking.

"It's not like that," her mother said standing tall, all emotions faded from her face. This was business now.

"It sounds pretty close," Amelia shot back. "Let me tell you how I see it, because really it's *all* about how *I* see it. I see you and Ambrose conspiring with Anatole. I see you all trying to make choices either for me or convince me to make the ones that best benefit you all, with little or no concern for me as a person.

"My feelings, my wants, my choices are not being respected. You promised me that you would accept my decisions, honor my free will, and you're changing up the playbook as we go along. And that is *not* ok with *me!*" Amelia finished, her gaze fixed on her mothers, challenging her. "If I feel like I want to change my mind I can. I can walk right out of here, forgetting all about you, about this place, and return to my normal boring life back in Texas."

"You can," her mother said shrugging. She was calling Amelia's bluff. But the thing is, her mother already knew what Amelia was feeling. Already knowing because of her gift, that she had decided to Unbind, already felt her thinking seriously about what was offered last night.

You couldn't play poker with a woman who had to gift of knowing your most secret feelings.

Amelia wanted to scream in frustration. She wanted to have the courage to walk out and not look back. And then she thought about Michelle, about how her decision would impact both her and Robert. How her decision could potentially impact them all, and the Larougo pack too. She felt instantly weighted down.

"Why does all this have to fall on me?" she said aloud, the tears of her frustration and lack of control taking her over the edge.

"I'm so sorry," her mother said, brushing the hair from off her face and behind her shoulders. She was back to her kind and motherly self, as Amelia struggled to control her emotions.

"What do I do?" she pleaded.

"I told you I would support whatever you chose, and I still stand by that. But, may I tell you why I think you should at least consider Anatole's proposition?"

Amelia just nodded as she sat, with her knees pulled up to her chest. She didn't even have the energy to stand anymore.

"I'm the last person who would champion a union between my daughter and one of their pack. After all the heartbreak, and the damage that one impulsive decision caused all those years ago. But I do know that Lachlean's death was avenged. I know that Anatole and the pack tried to undo what had been done. But Anatole, despite being gruff at times is a better leader than his father ever was. He's open to change.

"As for Roan, I've known him for twenty-some years now, and he's grown into a good man. That I can tell you. This union would be a way to solidify our allegiance. We would become the first group of Larougo and Garkain to combine and live together as one Colony. It would be a step into the future. We would rule side by side, Anatole, your grandfather, and myself.

"It would also be another way to right the wrong that was done when you were born. Justice for your father, and for me. To see you continue on his legacy and his bloodline." Amelia looked into her mother's eyes. She didn't want to say no.

"Where's Michelle?" Amelia asked.

"I just saw her. Why?" her mother asked.

"It has to be family to perform the ritual, right? I want Michelle to do it," Amelia said, standing.

"It *does* have to be family, but usually it's a direct descendant, a mother or father who breaks the mortal tether," her mother explained.

"Usually, but not always," Amelia picked up on her careful wordage.

"Correct," her mother said smiling. "Michelle would have to be first though. Only one who is Unbound can Unbind. That's usually why it's done by an elder."

"Well, I guess we'd better get going. You said the schedule had changed? That today and tomorrow the rituals would be held."

"Yes, but we'd have to ask Michelle if she would be okay with this," her mother said glancing around the room. Catching Michelle's eye, she waved her over, Michelle moving quickly to join them.

"Can we talk?" Amelia asked her sister, jumping in before her mother had the chance.

"Sure," Michelle said, with uncertainty lacing her voice.

Amelia led her back to their tent, keeping her voice low. "I'm going to do it," she told Michelle as they ducked inside, closing the flaps behind them.

"What? Do what?" Michelle asked, as she stared wide-eyed at her sister.

"All of it. The ritual, the marriage. I'm going to agree to it all."

"Whoa, wait. Are you crazy? You've had like a day, not even a day, to think about this, and you're sure this is what you want to do? Look, take more time, don't let anyone pressure you. You and I haven't really gotten the chance to talk about it anymore yet," Michelle pleaded with Amelia. "You said just last night that you needed more time. Time to think and to sleep on it."

"Yes and I did think, and I did sleep. But it makes sense. The more and more I think about it, the more it doesn't seem so bad. If it means a new beginning, a chance to be progressive, to do away with some of the things that are wrong and backward, then it's worth it. Or worth the chance anyway."

"Amelia, really, you don't have to do this," Michelle said again, driving home her point. "Wait at least until tomorrow?"

"No. No, it's okay. It's the right thing to do. And to be honest. I never wanted to go back to the States anyway. When I came here, I was hoping for a fresh start. Or the possibility of one at least. I didn't expect quite all this," she laughed waving her hand around. "But it's okay. It's better than the life I had back home. It's better than being a part of a family that doesn't want you. And hey, I could hang out with you for an eternity."

Michelle reached out pulling her sister in for a tight hug. "I'm with you, whatever you choose. You know that," Michelle said pulling back. "But I have to ask you about the big elephant in the room. Roan."

"The fact that he's gorgeous doesn't hurt, of course. Yes, you were right, there was no way not to notice. But beside the good looks, he seems intelligent, and kind of sweet. You were the one who just last night told me about how you liked him as a person," she reminded her, the blush coming back as she thought about him.

"Yeah, I kind of noticed the chemistry. And the fact that you couldn't stop looking at him without blushing. Like now," Michelle smiled.

"Stop it! Okay, so say it doesn't work, that I'm pure Garkain, then this whole thing never even has to happen anyway. And if we end up not getting along, he's dingo during the day and only human at night which means we'll barely even see each other.

"So . . . I have a favor to ask," Amelia said.

"Anything."

"I want you to perform the Unbinding. On me."

"Okay . . . I mean yes, of course. But why me?" Michelle asked.

"Because I trust you. And because I know you'll take me through it step by step, gently."

"That means that I'll have to Unbind first," Michelle said.

"Right, and that's the other thing. I'd like us to do it today. Now."

A look of hesitation passed over Michelle's face. Something Amelia didn't expect. She'd thought that Michelle was ready, would be happy to Unbind as quickly as possible. But she supposed that, even when you've been brought up in a culture where death is a rite of passage, the actual act of dying was a scary idea for anyone. Even her.

"Let's go talk to mother," she smiled and stood. They headed out into the great room again, looking for their mother and Ambrose, who were standing together, deep in conversation as they made their way toward them.

"Mother," Michelle said, calling her attention from Ambrose. And if Amelia wasn't mistaken, she heard her name as they were walking up. They'd been talking about her.

"Amelia and I have decided that we will Unbind today. I will go first, and once I complete the ritual, I will be the one to Unbind her."

Her mother and Ambrose both nodded. "We were just discussing that, and Ambrose is willing to bend the rules a little for you both. Robert will also need to agree to be Unbound at the same time as Michelle. We're looking for him now," her mother explained.

"And there he is. Robert my boy, I trust you've been enjoying yourself, considering no one's seen you come out of the tents," Ambrose teased him. For the first time since she met him, Robert actually had a smile on his face.

"You could say that," he shot back.

"Your sisters have decided to be the first to Unbind today. But you'll also have to agree, as you know."

"Not a problem here, I've been waiting on *her* for years," he said nodding at Amelia, then shooting her a smile. She still hadn't made her mind up about him yet. But as her brother, she wanted to like him. Seeing him smile was nice.

"It's settled then. Tonight, my dear children, you will leave behind your mortality, and take your place in the

Colony," Ambrose told them with a smile of pride on his face. "And Amelia, have you decided, should you be both Garkain and Larougo what your answer will be to Anatole's proposition?"

"Yes, I have. I will accept his offer. On one condition," she said causing Ambrose to raise an eyebrow. "We will live here. Roan and me. Because of our, um, differences, we can't live in the city. But we can build a home here. Or near here rather," she said. It only seemed fair. If they were to be partners, as Anatole asked, they would need a home. And the only way she saw it working was to build one here.

Ambrose wasted no time in his decision. "We will start as soon as the Celebration ends, within three months, you and Roan will have a home. Together," he said with a broad smile.

"Thank you," she said.

"Okay, three hours from now will be nightfall, and the ritual can begin," Ambrose said, walking away and leaving Phoebe with her children.

"And I'm coming to visit, once a week," Michelle said embracing her sister again.

"Done!" Amelia agreed.

"Amelia, I'm proud of you," her mother said, giving her a brief and awkward hug.

Michelle and Amelia wandered away from the group to talk a bit more before the rituals began.

"What do you think you'll miss most about being human?" Amelia asked.

"I don't think I'll miss much. Really. I think I'm more worried about becoming Garkain. Learning how to control your strengths and the gift. About learning how to feed, and blend in. About having to be so secretive all the time. But I'm also excited about the same things. It's tough to explain.

"I've spent my whole life preparing for this, so I know what to expect. I shouldn't be this nervous, but I am. A little. More nervous about Unbinding you now more than anything," she said.

"Sorry, but I trust you. It's that intuition or whatever, but I think you're the one that's supposed to do it. It just feels right for some reason. And all the other stuff you're worried about, I am too. I still have to go back to the States and close up my life there. Not to mention, the uncertainty of what I'll be like after.

"There's a lot of fear for me too. Don't let this cool exterior fool you. Inside, I'm freaking out!" she said trying to laugh and put them both more at ease.

"So, when this all happens, we'll be there for each other, right?" Michelle asked.

"Exactly. We'll figure it out together," Amelia agreed.

"If you don't mind though, I'd like to spend some time with my kids for a while," she said.

"No, of course! I'm going to hang out in here, try and get my head around all of this for my last few human hours," Amelia smiled as Michelle ducked out of the tent, leaving her alone.

The hours flew by, faster than she realized. As Amelia thought about her future and her past, and the choices she'd made that led her here. She was ready to commit to this new life.

Michelle pulled open the tent flap, nervousness radiating from her as she looked at Amelia sitting up on the cot.

"It's time," she said, leading the way into the main cavern. Leading them both to their deaths.

UNBINDING

The time she'd spent alone, had helped. She ran through all the information that she had put together, knew what to expect from some of the things she'd been told, and she was ready. Ready for whatever came next. Or as ready as she'd ever be. There was no turning back, and it was useless to be afraid. There was only one way out alive now, and that was by dying.

She followed Michelle, who's children had been safely hidden away with the other children in one of the tents. She could hear them laughing as someone told a story, distracting them from the events in the main hall.

She could imagine that even having grown up in the Colony, any child would have a hard time watching their mother or father die in front of them.

The chairs that she had seen before at breakfast were set out again. Two of them. One for Michelle and one for Robert, who took their places. Robert calmer than Michelle, who's face betrayed the hesitation which still lingered, as Ambrose wrapped a strap around both their chests. She watched carefully as two bags of blood were pulled from the refrigerator.

Ambrose, always the showman, stepped in front. "Tonight, we welcome three new members of not only the Colony but of the Royal bloodline. My bloodline," he said stepping aside.

Pulling off the top of the bag, both Michelle and Robert forced down their mothers' blood. She remembered what one of the girls had said, about this being the hardest part. She noticed them both resist the urge to gag. But slowly they sipped until the bag lay empty on their laps.

Her mother stepped beside Amelia, to help explain as the process continued. "Now they must wait for a few minutes until my blood starts to seep into their hearts," she whispered.

One of the women from earlier, the same one who had taken Michelle's blood over breakfast, stepped in taking her arm again and inserting the catheter inside the crook of her other elbow. As soon as the bag was attached, Phoebe came forward and started the letting processes. The bags began to fill quickly with both Robert and Michelle's blood.

"It will take a little more than four full bags to complete the letting. So this part will take a few minutes," Ambrose said coming up behind Amelia, as Phoebe continued to stay with Robert and Michelle, grabbing their hands for reassurance.

"How are you feeling?" he asked with genuine concern.

"I haven't changed my mind, if that's what you're asking," Amelia said, meeting his gaze.

"No, I'm asking how you're feeling," he said placing his hand gently on her shoulder.

"Nervous, but resolved," she said as he smiled at her.

Bag after bag was changed until they came to the fourth and final one. She noticed both Michelle and Robert beginning to look pale, deathly, their heads becoming heavier and heavier. Their eyes closing and struggling to remain open. Their mother stayed by their side the whole time.

As the fourth and final bag was full and removed, all of them were labeled, and put in the refrigerator for safekeeping. She noticed both her brother and sister had stopped moving completely. There was no subtle rise and fall of their chests, no fluttering of eyelids. No signs of human life at all.

The nurse returned, feeling for a pulse in their neck, then putting her stethoscope against Michelle's chest. She nodded, and Michelle was carefully unstrapped from her chair, her limp body laid carefully on the ground. The nurse moved next to Robert and the same was done. Both brother and sister lay side by side on the ground. Unmoving. Dead.

Her mother waved to Amelia to come and join her next to their bodies. "Now we wait," she whispered.

"How long?" Amelia asked.

"It varies, the longest I've seen was four hours. On average it could be between one to two hours," she said with a smile, trying to comfort Amelia's growing anxiety.

Time passed slowly, and again Amelia felt uncertainty creep into her mind. The longer they stayed dead, the more and more worried she became.

"Look," Her mother said, pointing to Michelle's hand. A finger moved, then another. Her mother reached out taking Michelle's hand as her eyelids began to flutter. "Hi, my darlings," she cooed, moving to sit in between them both as Robert's eyes also opened. "Take it slow. Slowly. Magda, blood please," she called for the nurse, who brought three pints for each of them.

Robert was the first to sit upright, his eyes seeming sensitive to the light, as he kept squinting and blinking. Shaking his head, as if trying to wake up.

Their mother helped them both drink down the first pint, which was taken much differently than it had been in the beginning, when they were still Bound. Now they were hungry. Drinking the other two bags quickly, taking in more human blood to give them strength.

As they finished, both Ambrose and their mother helped them to their feet. Their stance was unsteady, their feet shuffling, as life-giving blood returned to their muscles and veins. Their color began to come back, no longer pale with death. Amelia stared in awe as they began to come fully back around. Moving slowly at first then taking more steady steps, until they were just like they were before.

Amelia tried to run to Michelle's side, her mother holding her back. "Just a minute Amelia, stay back a bit," she warned. Michelle's face seemed to change, then she screamed out as her lips pulled back, revealing two sharp fangs protruding from behind her side canines, just as her mother's had in the hotel that day.

"You're still human. And she's still hungry. Come with me," Ambrose said, pulling her away from her sister, whose eyes welled with tears of apology. "She'll need more and more blood until the thirsting is gone. Give her an hour or so, and she'll be fine," he said trying to calm her.

Amelia stared from a safe distance as the nurse brought more blood for them. They were both led to the tent closest to the entrance. Now she understood all too clearly why children, especially hers, were kept occupied and elsewhere.

It was unnerving to think that she would have to go through the same loss of control. She knew that Michelle wasn't herself at the moment. And if she were truly as special as everyone treated her, she wondered what it might be like for her.

Having seen the ritual completed, she was relieved to know that she would come back. But also, she was more nervous about the transformation process, which seemed uncomfortable to say the least.

She stood frozen, thinking again. Yes, she was worried. And she could understand why Ambrose and Anatole were too.

Word must have spread that Amelia would be next, as one by one, other Colony members came by to give their congratulations and well wishes. Politely, she thanked them. Some introduced themselves, some didn't. She remembered none of their names. She was thoroughly focused on the tent by the entrance.

Again, the waiting. She'd finally made her decision and it was taking forever. The more time she had to think, the more time her mind ran on overdrive. A hushed silence fell over the room, as she looked toward the tent, seeing not Michelle or Robert, but Anatole and Roan.

Ambrose must have let them know about her decision, she thought. Her nerves were now beyond control. As the pair strode towards her and Ambrose, she noticed again how attractive Roan was as he smiled.

"Are we late?" Anatole asked.

"Right on time actually," Ambrose said. "My other two grandchildren have just Unbound, and Amelia will be next. She's also decided to accept your proposal. Conditionally."

"And what condition would that be?" Anatole asked with skepticism as he raised his eyebrows.

"A home. Here. Near both the Colony and your pack," Ambrose explained.

"That seems fair and generous," Anatole said. It appeared that her terms were agreeable to both sides.

"How do *you* feel about it?" It was Roan who asked Amelia. He seemed genuine in his caring about her feelings, which she hadn't expected.

"I feel, scared, nervous. I feel like it's the right thing to do. As your father said when we spoke, it's something that could be beneficial for both our people. I warn you though, I may not be easy to live with," she said in a mock warning, trying to lighten the heavy mood.

"Well if it makes you feel any better, I promise not to pee on the furniture," he smiled at her, making her smile too. Okay, she thought, this might just work.

The conversation in the hall had picked up again as all eyes turned toward the entrance. Michelle and Robert had emerged, along with their mother. "Amelia," her mother called, waving her over.

Roan put his hand on her back, as she started forward, making her turn around. "Be careful," he said. Oh yeah, this was going to work out *just* fine.

Amelia slowly walked toward her family, her senses on high alert. They seemed fine. Michelle was even smiling. "I'm ok, I promise. I'm so sorry about earlier," her sister said with regret. She wanted to hug her, but fear sparked inside, telling her to stay a few feet away.

"It's fine. But are you sure you can do the ritual with me? If not, I understand. I'm not so scared anymore. Well, not scared of dying. How does it feel?" Amelia asked.

Michelle thought for a minute before answering. "It feels amazing. And different. The lights take some getting used to. It's scary at the very beginning when you wake up. You can feel that something's missing. That you're dead. Which is pretty freaky. And the hunger is, well you saw. It's overpowering. It just takes a little while to get used to your new self. I feel fine now. Honestly," she said.

"And yes, I can do the ritual. The ritual wouldn't bother me. My part is easy. All I have to do is give you my new Garkain blood. The nurse does most everything anyway, as you saw. If you changed *your* mind, I wouldn't blame you, I wouldn't be upset if that's what you're worried about," she said.

"No, that's ok. I'd rather you do it, but it's completely up to you," Amelia said. She hated asking Michelle to do something she may not feel comfortable with, especially after just going through the Unbinding herself.

"Let's do it," Michelle said, heading off to the chairs, one for Michelle to give blood, and one for Amelia to go through the ritual.

The crowd formed again as the sisters took their places. This time there were no murmurs among the others, no gossip, as they simply stared and waited.

The nurse took Michelle's new blood, filling a bag quickly, then taking out the needle. Michelle handed Amelia the bag, then stood back as Ambrose strapped her into the chair, as he had done for Michelle and Robert.

She raised the bag to her lips. The first taste was, as she expected, a little off-putting. Like a liquid penny in her mouth. She took a deep draught and found that she was able to keep it down, but barely. Pride, and not wanting to gag in front of Roan, kept her steadily drinking until the bag was empty. She was a little nauseous, but fine otherwise.

She could feel it though, the blood. Not just in her stomach but warming her from the inside. Flowing through her as it made its way into her system. She felt a sudden rush, her eyes were already more sensitive, her hearing already more acute.

"How do you feel?" Ambrose asked as a select crowd formed. Most of the crowd was hanging back, Amelia noticed. Her mother, Michelle, Roan, Anatole, and

Ambrose however, all hovered. Eager and anxious with anticipation.

"Warm. I can feel it, the blood, I can feel it moving through my body. My eyes are a little sensitive too," she said, trying her best to describe what she felt as it happened. "I feel stronger. A little lightheaded. Is this how you felt?" she asked Michelle who didn't answer but looked toward her mother.

Before she could answer the nurse had already inserted the catheter and connected the tube to the bag, as Michelle quickly rolled back the stopper, letting Amelia's blood flow into the bag, which was filling up fast.

She could feel their emotions, nearly see them, she felt them so clearly. They were worried. Her mother was right. Her gift was like hers. Emotional. Empathic. Everything seemed to be hitting her at once.

"What's wrong? Somethings wrong. I can tell," Amelia said, her voice betraying the fear and worry that coursed through her along with the blood.

"We knew you'd react differently, or that you could. It appears that you're Unbinding now, between stages. Just try to calm down Amelia, please," her mother tried to reassure her. But Amelia knew she was lying and trying to hide the fact that she was scared. Scared of Amelia.

"How many bags is that?" Amelia asked.

"Four. You should be out soon, or getting sleepy, how do you feel now?" Ambrose leaned in to ask.

"The same. Maybe more sensitive to the light. It's so bright. It's killing my eyes. And can you speak a little softer, it sounds like you're yelling." Amelia tried to grab her ears to block out the noise, but her hands were restrained. She squeezed her eyes shut against the light.

"She's Unbinding while she's dying, it's happening at the same time," Roan said stepping in. "Amelia, can you look at me. Look at me," he coached soothingly. She tried to open her eyes, feeling how concerned he was. How truly worried he was about her right now.

"Pupillary response is insane, something I've never seen before. All her senses are getting a double shot of sensitivity. Iris color is nearly reflective. She's taking in everything times two," he said in a clinical way.

"Can you be quieter, please? Please can everyone just be quiet? Can you turn off the lights can you just, please stop this. I don't want to do this anymore. I can't take it anymore. I can't, I . . . ." She stopped mid-sentence as her head hung down. A full five and a half pints of blood and she had finally passed out, severing her mortality.

Ambrose and the others held their places for a few minutes, gauging the situation. The nurse came by, performing the same basic check for respiration and heartbeat as she did for Robert and Michelle, before Ambrose untied her and gently carried her straight to the recovery tent.

They had already witnessed something different than any Unbinding before. They had no idea what to expect once Amelia awoke.

Only Ambrose, Roan, and Anatole were allowed into the tent. The others waited patiently outside. A safe distance away.

"I think it's safe to say that she's definitely different?" Anatole asked Ambrose, who nodded.

"I would say so," he agreed. "How she'll wake up is anyone's guess at this point."

The trio sat patiently waiting. As the hours stretched on, and still no signs of movement, a hushed and worried tone fell over the entire Colony. Complete failure was the least likely outcome. But it was one that could potentially happen.

"How long now?" Roan asked for the second time.

"Four hours and counting," Ambrose said, looking at his watch, and the six pints of human blood on standby, just in case.

Amelia's eyes fluttered, then flashed wide open. She sat up screaming, pulling at her mouth, blinded by agony, and completely confused.

Ambrose reached for the first bag, holding it out to her as she gulped it down mouthfuls at a time.

"Another," she demanded, all civility and politeness gone. He handed over two, which she also gulped down. More and more bags lay empty on the ground until she'd finished them all, the last two a bit slower.

It seemed as if she were coming back to her surroundings, taking in everything, but still keeping her eyes squeezed tightly shut against the light.

"Amelia, can you hear me? What do you feel right now? Try and be as specific as possible," Anatole asked.

"Irritated by the same question on repeat," she shot at him. "My gums hurt, my mouth hurts, my whole jaw is killing me," she moaned.

"That's your new teeth breaking through at the smell of human blood," Ambrose jumped in.

"Can we, would you mind if I looked?" Roan asked kindly.

Amelia leaned back pulling her mouth wide revealing two sets of teeth. One set Garkain, just behind the canines. But the canines too had changed. Two rows of piercing teeth in one spot.

"Double canines, it's no wonder your mouth hurts," Roan explained. "What about your senses, sight, sound, feelings?" he probed for more information.

"I can barely stand to open my eyes. Everything is so bright it's miserable. And every sound is deafening, but it's not as bad as it was before.

"Feelings. I feel strong. Really strong. I can feel what you're feeling. And that you like me, care about me. I can tell," she said losing her filter and looking at Roan who gave her a gentle and reassuring smile.

"You think I'm dangerous," she told Anatole, whipping her head in his direction. "And you. I have no idea what you're thinking," she said to Ambrose. It was like trying to feel through a wall. There were feelings there, she could sense them, she just couldn't get through to them.

"I'm happy you woke up and worried about what your combined gifts will mean," he admitted. She sensed he was telling the truth, but she couldn't be positive without a good read.

Amelia groaned, forcing her eyes to stay open, to try and adjust to the light. "Ugh, the light is still too bright, but I think my eyes are getting used to it. Maybe," she said.

Roan leaned in, "Let me see," he said softly. "They're changing. The longer you keep them open, the darker your irises are becoming. It's a similar reaction for the eyes to light, as it is for your skin to the sun. Fascinating," he mused. "The longer you keep them open, the less sensitive they should become. Are you still hungry?" he asked.

"Yes, kind of. Not like before. I can wait," she said, swinging her legs around and putting them on the ground. "Whoa," she said as the room spun for a moment.

"Slowly," Ambrose said.

She held her head in her hands for a moment, opening her eyes and forcing them to focus on the tip of her boot, trying to stop the spinning.

"Roan, would you mind staying with Amelia, while Ambrose and I have a word?" Anatole asked.

"No, not at all," Roan replied happily.

He sat quietly with her on the cot as the two Elders exited the tent. "They're worried," Amelia said softly.

"They're just trying to make sense of what's going on. Someone like you has never been seen before. And I don't know if you remember the Unbinding. But, let's just say that it was unusual. You're unique in so many ways," he said, trying to sound supportive and positive.

She focused in on the conversation outside, hearing it perfectly through the canvas. "She's dangerous," Anatole told Ambrose. "But she's controlling it, acclimating quickly. There's no reason to consider culling her. She'll be fine. Roan will stay with her if you'd like. This is what we had hoped for, both Garkain and Larougo genetics," Anatole was reasoning with Ambrose.

"We'll give her the next two days. Observe her closely. And yes, Roan is welcome to stay with her, if that's what you're requesting. I think that would be a comfort to her," Ambrose said.

"And someone of the Larougo bloodline may be able to help her navigate those specific feelings and attributes. She has you and your family to help navigate becoming Garkain, but no one from our pack," Anatole said.

"You make a valid point."

"And being that they are now officially betrothed, the more time they spend together, the better. Especially during this time for her," Anatole continued.

"That's fine. We have a small room usually for supplies, but we can clear that out. Give them some privacy," Ambrose considered.

"Then it's settled."

Inside the tent, Roan noticed Amelia concentrating, smiling, then frowning. "You can hear them, can't you?" he whispered. Amelia nodded.

"What are they saying?"

"Well, it looks like you're staying here for a while, to help me. And since we're going to be stuck together from now on, I guess I'd better find out now if I like you," she smiled.

"You mean if I like you?" he shot back, giving her the same snarky smile.

THE ROOM

It was small, to be sure. Intimate, which made her nervous. And her dislike of small spaces would have to take a backseat to the more important issues right now.

Whoever had arranged the small room had done their best to make it comfortable. Two individual cots, with a table in the middle and a single bulb hanging from the ceiling. Fresh covers for the beds and in the corner, someone had thoughtfully hung a canvas flap taken from one of the tents to form a kind of private space.

The room had all the small attention to details that would make Amelia feel more comfortable. If she had to guess, she would say Michelle had a heavy hand in the design. She said a silent thank you to her sister, instantly wishing they could talk.

But from the look of things, she was in isolation for now, at least until they were sure she wasn't dangerous. No visitors, other than Roan, who's feeling were coming through as clearly as a voice. He was downright uncomfortable at the moment. But to his credit, he didn't outwardly show it.

There was no door to the room, but a piece of plywood that fit perfectly over the open space, affording them sanctuary from the curious and prying eyes of the rest of the Colony. It also kept her contained. She wasn't naïve.

Just walking across the main hall to their room was a spectacle. So many comments that included either her or Roan's name. Thankfully she couldn't pick apart which comment came from which person as she felt her anger rising. The gossip was starting to really piss her off.

Inside the room and away from the noise, it was easier to focus her hearing on the quieter sounds, like their slow and steady breathing, or the burning of the filament inside the single bulb. She noticed that there had been more at one time, hanging along the cord on the ceiling, but that they had been thoughtfully removed. The lighting was dim and easier on her eyes. Again, she said a silent thank you to Michelle.

Anatole had left some time ago, Ambrose promising to keep him apprised of anything notable. Her things had been brought to their room, and some of the Colony members had generously donated a pile of things for Roan to use.

Alone together and struggling for conversation, awkward silence hung above them. "I'll have to leave here soon, the sun's about to be up," Roan said as Amelia sat down on her cot.

"Oh, of course. I completely forgot about that," Amelia said, embarrassed. "I'll be fine. I have my sister and my mother if I need them. But to be honest, I'm tired after the long night, and it's nice to have a place where I can be by myself. Not forced to socialize if I don't want to."

"I understand. Larougo are very social, but sometimes it's nice to be by myself," he paused. Waiting.

"Do you want to ask me anything before I leave? Anything about your Larougo side?" he asked, trying not to pry.

"Actually yes. Can I see your fingers? Or can you look at mine? Do I need to worry about that?" she asked. She tried not to think about how lightly he took her hand, or how amazingly sensitive his fingers on her skin felt to her now. Even her sense of touch was heightened, she noticed.

He moved her hands this way and that, looking under her fingernails, pressing gently on the nailbed. "I don't feel anything like mine, here, feel," he said, showing her where to press.

Under the skin where his nail met his finger was a slight hump. Running her fingers over it lightly she could feel it immediately.

Her head snapped up as a thought entered her mind. "Wait! I have to go with you, don't I? Do I? Am I going to change when you do, during the day?" she asked panicking. Another thing she hadn't thought of until now.

"That's a good question. I don't know, hold on," he said standing and moving to the door. "Ambrose!" he called out through the wooden door.

Within seconds her grandfather appeared, sliding the plank over just a bit. "What's wrong? What is it?" Amelia could finally get a read on him this time. Concern. So his grumpy ass did care, a little.

"Amelia brings up a good point. Considering that she most certainly has traits of both bloodlines, there is a possibility that she could turn come morning. Which should be soon," Roan said.

Ambrose looked at his watch. "About thirty minutes, I would say, and we'll find out," he said with trepidation.

"Okay, I have to leave anyway, as we discussed earlier. Let Amelia come with me to the door of the tunnel. Leave the door open. If she does turn, she can run with me. If not, I'll come back at nightfall, as promised," Roan said.

Ambrose considered the options for a moment, which were few at this point. His emotions flickered between fear, worry, and concern. "Alright, let's go. Quickly," he said, pulling back the door all the way, letting them out of the room.

Roan grabbed Amelia's hand, leading her to the tunnel entrance, ignoring the stares as they navigated through the crowd. They were jogging, close to running down the corridor. Waves of nervous energy flowed from Roan as they continued on. . .

"You better hurry, I can feel the sun," he called behind him.

They were close to the door as Amelia raced past him, twisting the handle, flinging it open. The iron door landed heavily against the outside ground, but to Amelia, it felt as light as a feather.

Roan dropped to his knees just short of the stairs. As he groaned, she heard what sounded like bones breaking, and skin tearing. She turned to see him contorted, transitioning. She gasped at the sight. A look of agony crossed his face as it began to change. His body covered in thin hair, growing thicker.

She did a physical inventory of herself, feeling her face, and running her hands over her smooth skin. She wasn't changing. At least she didn't think she was.

Roan continued his torturous transition, writhing as the sun from the East hit her eyes, causing her to seal them shut against its brightness.

All at once the sounds of pain subsided and she dared to squint into the light. She caught sight of Roan's dingo form as it shot past her into the day. She stood squinting and watching him run, waiting to see if anything might still happen to her.

Several minutes later, she turned back to the stairs. She grabbed the door from the ground and swung it over the top of her as she headed back into the ground. She made sure to secure it before heading back toward the heart of the Colony.

She was grateful for not having to change. She felt sympathy for Roan, who seemed to be in agony while he made his transition. She did check her fingernails again, and to her surprise, she now felt the small lump beneath the bed of her thumbnail. They were longer than they had been before too.

She also tasted blood. Feeling inside her mouth carefully, she did feel one set of sharp teeth. The ones in the front, not the Garkain teeth in the back.

As she slowly made her way, deep in thought, a shape caught her attention further down the tunnel. Ambrose, she realized, making sure everything was alright.

"Amelia?" he asked cautiously into the dark.

"It's me. I'm ok, I didn't turn," she said continuing on but not rushing. Even from this far away she heard him exhale and felt his relief.

"Roan is gone, I shut and secured the door behind him," she said as she passed him, on her way back to her room. She felt like being alone right now anyway. The only person she could have contact with was gone. It would be just her in the closet all day.

Ambrose let her pass without a word. Maybe he could sense her lack of wanting to talk right now. Whatever the case, she made it back to her room and pulled the wooden door back into place.

A wave of exhaustion hit her as she realized she hadn't slept since yesterday. If she calculated right, she'd clocked maybe six hours of sleep total for the two days. Not exactly well-rested. And she felt it.

She had to concentrate to block out the noises from the main chamber, but the wooden door helped a little. Because of the sheer exhaustion from both her time awake and the events of the past two days and nights, she fell into a deep sleep within minutes.

What must have been a gentle knock at the door sent her springing from her bed. Her first instinct was to hide, to press herself against the back wall. Some danger *she* was, she thought snidely.

"Who is it?" she said softly, as her ears adjusted.

"It's me, Michelle. Can I come in?" she asked cautiously.

"I think, I mean, it's okay with me. I'm okay," she stuttered.

Michelle slowly slid the door over just enough to squeeze herself through. Amelia squinted against the light from the great hall, streaming in through the crack.

"Eyes are still really sensitive, sorry," she said as she opened them again, blinking and letting them re-acclimate. Michelle hung by the door. An unmistakable wave of wariness emanated from her.

"I'm not going to hurt you," Amelia said.

"I know," she paused, then moved a little closer, sitting on the very end of the bed nearest the door. She was still guarded, scared, and cautious. "We haven't seen each other since you Unbound. I just wanted to check on you."

"A socially appropriate answer would be the typical 'I'm fine'. But honestly, I'm anything but fine. I'm really scared. And I know that Ambrose is too. He's hiding something. I can't feel his emotions like I can yours and everyone else's," she confided.

"Ambrose is rare. He's spent decades and more putting that wall in place. No empath can get through it. Not my mother, and not me, even now. You seem to have an even stronger gift than we do, and if you can't get through, no one can," she said simply.

"I can, a little, at times. He's worried and concerned. I think he does care what happens to me, or at least I feel he does. Can *you* feel what I'm feeling now?" Amelia asked her sister, a little afraid to hear what she would say.

"I can feel your fear. I know that you're scared about something. But you have a bit of a wall too. That could be the Larougo side of you. Garkain can't use our gifts on any of the Larougo pack. I can sense bits from you, but not a full feeling, it's like a fractured picture," Michelle said. "Everything is kind of half and half it seems. At least from what I've picked up from the conversations."

"What is everyone saying?" Amelia asked, not really sure if she actually wanted the answer or not.

"Mostly generic observations, about the Unbinding. How no one's seen anything like it. Speculations that you have superpower hearing, everyone's been whispering, thinking that you can hear and see through walls," she laughed. "Nothing bad, just idle gossip," she said with a face.

"Yeah," Amelia said. "That's kind of starting to get to me to be honest with you."

"I don't blame you, and believe me, I shoot them the evil eye when I hear them talking about you," she said smiling.

"There is something new. Here, let me show you," Amelia whispered, moving closer to Michelle and sitting in front of her. She felt her sister's anxiety skyrocket, her fight or flight response in overdrive. "I wish you weren't so afraid of me. It makes me sad," Amelia said as she started to tear up. Being close this whole time, she wondered if she'd ruined that, when Unbinding was only supposed to bring them closer together.

"I'm sorry, I can't help it. My emotions are on overdrive right now too," she said apologetically.

Amelia could understand that, but it still made her worry about their close bond that had formed. By becoming a part of the Colony, she never thought she might be risking her relationship with her sister.

"I get that, I do," Amelia said. "But I miss you, and I need someone to talk to. I feel like a freak. Like everyone is scared of me, and maybe they're right, I don't know. But I just feel . . . alone." Amelia let her emotions come through, tears running down her cheeks.

Michelle came to sit by her, hugging her close. "I'm not going anywhere I promise," she said.

"I have to show you something. I would ask Roan, but he's gone. Look . . .," Amelia said as she raised her pointer finger. "My nails are longer, and if you feel, right here, there's a gland. Under the skin like Roans." She held her finger out for her sister to touch.

Michelle flinched and pulled away. "Amelia don't tell anyone else about that. Okay? Trust me," she whispered, looking around.

Amelia's nerves were back in high gear as she moved closer to her sister, who kept inching away. "Why? What's wrong?" she asked, still keeping her voice low.

"It's a Larougo weapon, against us. It's also why we keep the door shut to the outside during our celebrations, and why Garkain live far away in the city. Just to err on the side of caution. Even though we have a truce, accidents have happened.

"That gland, at the base of your nail holds a poison. If it were to get into our blood it causes a terrible madness. Hallucinations, despair, pure terror. Most Garkain don't survive, and if they do, some effects are permanent. *That* is your most dangerous Larougo trait. The one they hoped you wouldn't get," Michelle said with gravity.

"Is there a cure? An antidote?" Amelia asked, pulling her hands back and tucking them under herself.

Michelle nodded. "The blood of the Larougo that injected the poison. But because the venom only appears when they're in dingo form, it's hard to tell who it was. From what I've been told, and you can ask Roan about this, they don't remember much about the days when they come back into human form. So even they can't tell who it might have been. Let's just keep this between us, ok?" Michelle said with a shy smile.

"I heard Anatole say something about this when we were alone the other night. That I may be immune and that if Roan and I were to have children, they may be too," Amelia said, thinking for a second.

"Hold on, and be quiet," she whispered as Michelle's eyes went wide.

"What are you doing?" she whispered.

"Shhh . . ." Amelia pulled her hands from under her. "How long before the madness sets in?" Amelia asked.

"I've never seen it happen myself. Only heard about it. But I think it's pretty quick, maybe immediate," she said.

"Let's see," Amelia said, quickly slicing through her wrist, drawing blood with her sharp nail.

"Are you crazy?" Michelle nearly said a little too loudly.

"We're about to find out," Amelia said as she stood and moved to the farthest wall again, sitting with her knees pulled to her chest. She looked down at her wrist, the wound completely healed up.

"Well that's interesting," she mused.

"Oh, we can't die, so our wounds heal right up. But not from a Larougo scratch. Not typically. Then again, you're not typical. Anything yet?" Michelle leaned a little closer as she kept her eyes steadily on Amelia.

"Wait, do you see the pink goblin in the corner too?" Amelia stifled a laugh as Michelle actually turned her head to look.

"Not funny, you brat," she said stifling a laugh of her own.

Amelia was glad they could get back to a less formal conversation. She did feel isolated in this room by herself. It was so nice to show Michelle that she was still the same Amelia. Or mostly the same, anyhow.

"I don't feel anything different," she said. "That's good, right?"

"I would take a chance and say yes. Considering everything so far has reacted slightly different with you, I'd wait to celebrate. And look, I'm technically supposed to be staying away from here, so I have to go before I get in trouble. You slept most of the day though, so Roan should be back pretty soon," Michelle said, standing up and taking a chance again. She walked over to Amelia, hugging her tight, then quietly snuck back out the door.

Amelia laid back down on her bed, looking around the room, waiting. Maybe she was immune. Hopefully Roan would know more about it, have more input. He seemed to know what he was talking about at least. She wished he would hurry up. She smiled, realizing, that she did miss having him here. A little.

After another hour or so of waiting, his voice came through clearly from the other side of the door. "Decent in there?" he said. Humor in his voice, and excitement in his emotions.

Amelia let herself smile. "Yes, I'm good. Come on in," she said. "Boy do I have something to tell you. Let's just say, I'm glad you're back." he moved in and hugged her tightly. And she really wished he didn't have to let her go.

NEW DISCOVERIES

"I'm happy to see you too," Roan laughed in her ear.

"Did you turn? I didn't see you," he asked excitedly.

"No, I didn't."

"Did you see me turn?" he asked with embarrassment. So the ripping was clothes, she thought and not skin. She tried to hide her blush as she was a little disappointed at not seeing a naked Roan, she realized to her surprise.

"Only the first part, the sun hit my eyes and I missed most of it," she said, trying to put his mind at ease. "But something did happen," she whispered. They both moved to the cots, sitting, facing each other, leaning in so they could be quiet. She felt his breath on her ear. Again, her sense of touch so heightened she felt a shiver move down her back.

"My nails grew, and the lump under the nail bed like yours, it happened to me too," she said. He pulled back looking at her. "And Michelle came to visit me. But that went fine. No hunger or anything, I was in control. But she told me more about the Larougo madness, the venom causes it, right?" she asked.

"Yeah, it's a toxin, it affects the brain. From what I can figure it's like a neurotoxin that takes over the central nervous system. It causes hallucinations and affects speech and motor skills. If a Garkain becomes infected they're usually spared the agony and culled."

"As in killed?" Amelia asked.

"It's preferable to enduring the effects of the toxin. Most Garkain beg for a merciful and quick end," he said.

"Michelle said there's a cure."

He nodded again. "But only if you can find the Larougo who infected you, which is usually a problem."

"Right, Michelle said that you don't always remember things after you turn, and that being in your dingo form, it's hard to tell who is who."

"She's right. But you don't need to worry about it, being here with them. If you don't turn like me, you won't have to worry about doing it on accident. Is that what you wanted to ask?"

"Well, kind of, but also about this . . ." she said holding up her wrist for him to see.

"I don't see anything."

"No, you don't because it healed. When it was daytime and the venom was in my nail, I slashed my wrist."

"You what?!" he said a little too loudly. Amelia could hear immediate quiet in the next room. She put her finger to her lips, then gestured outside and to her ear.

They waited for a while to see if anyone might investigate. Thankfully no one did.

"You're the scientist," she said looking at him and keeping her voice low. "I just experimented. Look, when your father talked to me, about, well, about us. He said that if we were to. . . If we happened to have children," she said blushing again. "He said that maybe they would have an immunity, which meant he thought that I might have an immunity once I Unbound. He was right."

"You should've waited for me. That was not smart Amelia," he said sternly.

Amelia shook her head, "I couldn't because by the time you came back it would have been night, and I would only be Garkain again. No venom, no nails." she flashed her hand for him to see.

"That was a risky thing to do," he chided her again. "Any effects that you can tell?"

"No, none. Nothing," she said smiling.

"I didn't know you were so brave."

"I have my moments," she said proudly.

"And I have a suggestion. My own experiment," he said.

"Okay, what's up?"

"Try to influence me."

"I can't, you're Larougo, Garkain can't use their gifts on Larougo. And besides, I haven't even practiced it yet. I don't know how."

"But you do have the gift, right? And it should be similar to your mother's if I'm guessing right. Empathic influencing?" he asked.

"I mean, yes, I would say it would be. I feel waves of emotions from people. Like you, you're happy and excited.

Earlier when Michelle came to see me, I could read her very clearly. She was afraid of me," Amelia said sadly.

"See? You shouldn't be able to read me at all, but you can. Maybe you can influence me as well. It's worth a shot, right?" he asked.

"I guess. What do you want me to influence you to do? And why do you trust me so much to let me go mucking around in your brain?"

"Because, if we're going to go through with the agreement you made to my father, trust is the most important part of any relationship. I have to trust you. Besides, you've given me no reason to distrust you so far."

"Okay, but if I get it wrong, don't be mad at me," she said.

"I promise. Okay, try and influence me to do something I wouldn't normally do. Let me think. Running naked through the Colony would probably get us both in trouble," he smiled.

"Probably, but then again you never know," she said with an evil grin.

"Let's not. How about, make me stand on my head, then do jumping jacks," he said.

"Do you trust me?"

"When you say it like that, I don't know if I do or not," he said laughing. "But until you prove me wrong, yes. I trust you."

"Okay, here goes nothing," she said.

Amelia closed her eyes, concentrating. She'd only seen her mother do this a handful of times. And only received a few brief instructions on how to. Her mother had influenced her several times, and she knew what that felt like. Hopefully she would get lucky.

She'd need to feel her way through it, without any help. She remembered how it felt to her, how she felt the emotions being triggered and shifted.

She locked on to his emotions. A bit of uncertainty had made its way in with the excitement. She delved deeper, looking for a feeling about her. And there is was. She could tell it was there, but it was something he tried to push down below, and not think about. But it was there. Attraction.

She smiled and latched onto that emotion. Then, using her concentration, she influenced him that beyond everything else, what he felt like wanting to do, was kiss her. A polite kiss. She re-evaluated the image in her thoughts that she was giving him.

She eased out of his mind, and out of her own concentration, opening her eyes. "Roan?" she whispered.

He opened his eyes and leaned toward her, staring at her, as she braced. His lips brushed against hers as they both closed their eyes again. His hand stroked her face, and she wished she had influenced him to kiss her in the way she had thought of before.

He pulled back, blinking. "Did it work?" he asked while Amelia giggled to herself. "What's so funny? What did you make me do?" But Amelia couldn't control herself. As hard as she tried, the laughter wouldn't stop.

"Okay, you didn't make me run around the Colony naked. Did you?" he asked as a look of pure terror crossed his face.

"No, no. I wouldn't do that," Amelia told him, pulling herself together. "I made you . . . kiss me," she said.

Now it was Roan's turn to burst out laughing. "You cheater! You went for something easy. I've wanted to do that since I first walked through the door earlier. I just hugged you. Didn't want to push my luck. Did you like it?" he said giving her his dark eyes.

"Eh, you're alright," she said, both of them laughing.

"Yeah, okay," he said, his ego slightly bruised. "Next time it'll be better."

"Next time?"

"Yeah, next time. *You* got to pick what kind of kiss it was. Next time I do," he grinned. "But we did learn that it works," he said, becoming a bit more serious.

"Yes, it worked. But when my mother first influenced me in the beginning, to stay calm, to not freak out. When she started telling me about all this. About the Colony, about Unbinding, I fought through it eventually. Or it started to fade. I don't remember exactly, but it didn't last past a day."

"Okay, so the same would probably be true for any Larougo. You could influence them short term, but not anything that required an extended period of time, which is kind of a disappointment," he said, thinking to himself.

"Why is that?" Amelia asked.

"Because I wanted you to try and influence me in the morning not to change."

"Oh."

"That would mean, no more wasted days. We wouldn't have to live out here. We could live in the city, or wherever the hell we wanted. And I could be with you all the time. Not just at night," he said.

"If you want, we can try it in the morning. We'll do the same thing as this morning, going to the door. I'll try to influence you and we'll see what happens," she said.

"And because tomorrow is your last day here, it's the last time we'll be able to try it. Do you know how frustrating it is to miss out on a normal life, day after day? I want to actually do things and experience life. If you could influence me, for long enough, I could even go back with you to the States. See what it's like." he reached out and grabbed her hands. "If that would be okay with you.

"Look, I know this whole agreement sounds crazy. And it probably is. I told you, I didn't agree with it at first either. But then I met you. And I liked you, and now it doesn't seem like a crazy idea at all. So, if we *are* going to do this. I want to give it our best shot. It's not worth trying to bluff your way through spending eternity together if you don't actually work to make it work."

"I agree," Amelia said.

"Okay, it's a deal. And tomorrow morning, we'll see how it goes."

"We'll see how it goes," Amelia said reaching out her hand, and shaking on it.

She'd slept most of the day away, leaving her wired that night. It was hard to sleep. Especially thinking about the next morning. She wanted to sneak out of the room and go tell Michelle. But she thought better of it and passed the time the best she could.

Ambrose knocked on the door at some point waking them both. She went to the door, sliding the plywood over. "Is everything ok?" she asked.

"Oh yes," he said clearing his throat. "Everything's fine. I just wanted to see if you'd like some breakfast. It's about an hour before sunrise, and I thought I could bring you both something."

"That sounds good, thank you," she said, as he quickly shuffled off. Another knock and she found a plate of actual food, for Roan, she guessed. And three full bags of blood for her.

She felt her mouth begin to burn, the teeth breaking through the skin with the taste of her own blood. She finished the first bag immediately, still kneeling by the door, then carried the plate and the other two bags to the cots. She handed Roan his plate first, then sat on her cot to finish her breakfast.

"Do you mind?" Roan asked. "I mean, could I take another look?"

Amelia stopped mid drink. "At what? My teeth?" she said immediately embarrassed. "I guess," she said opening wide.

Roan took his time looking this way and that. "Amazing, you are truly unique."

"Good or bad unique?" she asked.

"Good, definitely good," he smiled. Putting her at ease. She couldn't explain how the connection formed so quickly. Maybe being stuck in the same room together had something to do with it. But there was something else too.

A natural attraction she would have felt without any gift. Although the gift helped too.

"Well, when you're done, I'm ready if you are," he said, still sitting, waiting patiently for her to finish the last bag.

"All done," she said, tossing the empty bag on the cot with the others.

"Then let's see what happens," he said standing and reaching for her hand, pulling her to her feet.

They eased out of the room, keenly aware of the same stares as yesterday. She also noticed that there were fewer people in the main hall this morning. Maybe some had already left early. They all arrived together, but maybe they left at different times.

Starting down the corridor again, she was getting nervous. Influencing someone to give you a light kiss was one thing. But, trying to keep them from shifting, was quite another. She didn't want to fail him in something so important.

At the door, she looked back listening for Ambrose or anyone who might have followed them, but she heard nothing. They were alone. She had proved she could handle Roan with his transition yesterday, and she assumed that was good enough for Ambrose.

"I'm ready," he said, staring deep into her eyes and then closing them.

She used the same process, sensing her way through his mind. If she could find a feeling of having to turn or needing to turn, maybe she could influence that. She probed as deep as she could, past feelings that made her sad, feelings that made her happy, and feelings that made her angry.

Something this base, this instinctual would be deep. Very deep.

At last, she found something, possibly something that she could work with. A feeling of duty, of accepting the change as part of who he was. She reached out, carefully sifting through the other feelings to isolate just this one.

Modifying this feeling was not an easy task, each way she pushed or pulled, it sprang back into form. She had to think quickly, the sun was nearly up. She tried one final thing, giving him the feeling that she would be sad if he turned, that she didn't want to spend the days without him. It was an honest feeling, and that was the one that seemed to stick.

She pulled back out of his mind, careful to leave the other feelings in place as she slowly pulled herself up through his consciousness and back out again. She opened her eyes, seeing his still closed.

"Roan?" she said, reaching out to brush the hair from his eyes. He was sweating, but his eyes didn't open. She waited for a few minutes before speaking again. "Roan, come on, please wake up," she begged, wondering how long she'd spent trying to find that feeling.

Finally, his eyes opened as he shook himself awake, out of the trance-like state. "Are you okay? I had to go deep, really deep. I was afraid you weren't going to come out of it," she said, reaching out and hugging him. "Are you okay? Roan, say something," she demanded.

"I will if you let me get a word in," he said smiling. "I feel fine, a little bit of a headache, which I haven't had since I first transitioned. So, whatever you did had some effect."

He moved past her and up the stairs, reaching for the handle to the door. With a twist of the knob, he pushed his way through, holding it up for Amelia to walk out with him. He gently closed the door after them, looking off in the direction of the glow in the East.

"We'll know in about five minutes, I can feel the sun, I always feel it when it's close," he said sitting on the ground and taking her hand. She leaned into him as they sat and watched the sun break over the horizon. Both remaining themselves, Roan still in his human form.

"Thank you," He said as emotions of relief and joy radiated from inside him.

He brushed the hair from her face, causing her to turn as she squinted against the growing light. And this time he didn't kiss her gently.

THE NEW DEAL

They stayed that way for nearly an hour, sitting in the sun. Amelia watched as her skin began to blotch and darken, like her mothers and the other Garkain. Roan gently stroked her skin as it changed.

As they sat, Amelia forced herself to keep her eyes open longer and longer until they finally adjusted to the bright sunlight. It was uncomfortable but bearable.

"How do they look now," she asked Roan for the hundredth time.

"Still beautiful, and still the same dark blue," he said nudging her playfully. "Are you going to remember all this?" she asked.

"I hope so," he said with a smirk. "Actually, I remembered the kiss. I just didn't tell you."

"Why didn't you say something?" she pulled back looking at him.

"Because, I don't know. I didn't want you to be embarrassed maybe. I should have told you. But the look on your face was kind of worth it," he teased as Amelia gave him a look.

"So, we can say that it worked. Officially," she said, changing the subject.

"It did work, the only question is now, for how long? You said your mother's influence wore off after a few hours, so the same might happen to me," he said.

"Well, even if it does, it means that for a little while at least, you can be human during the day. And we can keep track of how long it lasts. Maybe we can keep doing it through the day if we have to," she suggested.

"You'd do that?" he asked.

"Of course. I hated watching you turn like that. I could hear your bones breaking. I can't even imagine what you must have to go through each time. It must be agony."

"It is. But it gets better over time. My first time was the worst. It took almost an hour to make the first transition. Each day got better and better. Now, it's a lot quicker. But it's still as painful as you think it is. Thankfully it just doesn't last as long," he said.

She heard footsteps from underground, still far away, but getting closer. "Someone's coming," she said. "They probably noticed when I didn't come back."

"Well, I suppose we'll have a chat with Ambrose. I would guess that it's him."

The door inched open, Ambrose's deep voice calling out. "Amelia?"

"Yes, I'm here. We're here," she clarified.

"We? Is Roan with you?" he asked, his voice laced with caution.

"Yes, but he's human," she answered.

The door flew open, as Ambrose took a step or two, his head appearing above the opening into the ground, still cautious. He looked around until his eyes found them, sitting under one of the trees, painted in sunlight.

"It's fine Ambrose. I'm still me," Roan called to him, as he kept climbing, standing on the ground, and walked toward them slowly.

"How is this possible?" he stared in shock.

"Amelia. She did it. She can influence me not to turn. This means that she can influence all Larougo. Or it's a potential possibility. And don't worry she didn't do it without me asking her to. Begging her to, actually," Roan said.

"Have you told your father?" Ambrose asked.

"No, the sun is up, he's not in human form now. We can tell him tonight," Roan offered.

"I was wondering about your gift," Ambrose said. "And you've been able to do something that's never been done before. At least not to my knowledge.

"They're all leaving here today, but I've decided to stay until tonight. I need to speak to your father as well. We all should.

"If you're able to, you can fly back to the city with us. If Amelia is agreeable, of course. And your father. But for now, keep this to yourselves. You can go around to the back of the rock, there are caves that you can hide in. I'd rather not spread this around just yet. Do you understand?" he asked.

"Of course," Roan answered for them, getting to his feet and pulling Amelia up with him.

"Thank you. I will see you at sunset. Oh, and I brought these for you, Amelia," he said pulling two bags of blood from his jacket pocket.

"We'll see you at sunset then, and please tell Michelle that I'll see her soon," she said, as they took off in a jog. After a few minutes of searching, they found a niche in the rock where they could stay for a while.

"Did he seem nervous to you?" Amelia asked when they were settled against the wall.

"A little, but I'm not the one with the empathic gift, and from the way he made it sound, you have the strongest gift he's come across yet. So, you tell me."

Amelia shook her head. "I can't always read him. Michelle said that he's spent years learning how to put up a wall, kind of like a shield. I'm guessing so that my mother and other empaths can't read him. I've been able to break through a few times, but briefly."

"I couldn't really get a sense of him either, but he said he needed to talk to my father," Roan said.

"Any idea what about?" Amelia asked.

"Not a clue. I guess we wait until sundown."

"Oh yeah! Take a look at my nails," Amelia said, holding out her hand for Roan to examine. Just as he did last time, he looked under her nails, pressing on the beds of them.

"You're right, there's something there."

"And watch," she said, slashing into her skin again, leaving a gash which healed nearly instantly. "Nothing," she said proudly, flashing her arm for him to see.

"That is absolutely amazing and disgusting," he marveled. "Larougo wounds don't heal on Garkains. They heal when we happen to go against each other, unless it's a fight to the death, which is rare. But never against a Garkain. It must be your Larougo side," he explained as he grabbed her arm to look more closely.

"Ooh, you do it to me," she said excitedly.

"Yeah, I think I'll pass."

"Why not? You're here if I need help, and I'm already immune to myself. Let's see if it's an across the board immunity. For science," she said playfully.

Roan flashed his fingers for her. "No nails," he said pouting.

"But the venom glands are still there day and night, so you just need to get your venom into my blood," she said.

"I guess, but really Amelia, we don't have to take risks we don't need to."

"I know, but you've got me curious now. And it would be important for us to know for sure."

She carefully and slowly sliced through her other arm, holding open the skin so he could put his nails inside. She didn't feel any pain, but his fingernails brushing against her ligaments was a little strange.

"Okay, but if this goes badly, don't say I didn't try to talk you out of it."

They sat for a while both staring at each other in anticipation.

"Anything?" Roan said with a yawn after a while.

"Nope, nothing. I feel totally fine."

"Well, I guess that's settled then. You're immune to the venom, and I'm able to be influenced." His eyes shot wide.

"Amelia, you're strong, as in a special way strong. You have abilities that shouldn't exist and haven't before. You have all the benefits and none of the drawbacks. What if . . . What if my dad sees you as a threat? Or Ambrose?" Fear radiated from him, making Amelia nervous.

"But I'm not," she said.

"But you could be. Look, the influencing thing is already out there. Ambrose already knows, so there's no way to hide that. But for now, let's keep this our secret."

"Michelle said the same thing," Amelia said.

"Michelle knows? Who else knows?" he was growing irritated with her.

"No one else, just you and her. That's it. And she won't say anything. I know she won't."

"Okay. But just let's hold off on spreading around stuff like that for now," he said in a serious tone.

"I will," Amelia said, feeling like she'd just gotten in trouble.

As the sun dipped lower in the sky, she kept checking on Roan, who continued to doze as the day wore on, but still retained his human form. She'd heard plane after plane take off all afternoon. But the last one was over an hour or so ago. Ambrose would be coming for them soon.

"Roan," she whispered. His head lolled to the side as his eyes blinked open.

"Hmmm, sorry about that, this is usually my time to sleep. I'm going to have to get used to a new schedule now, I guess," he laughed.

"I haven't heard a plane in a while, which probably means Ambrose will be coming soon. How do you feel?"

"I still feel good. I feel like . . . I made you happy by not turning. Is that weird? *I* feel happy that I didn't have to turn," he said.

Amelia's head whipped around as she heard something far off, in the distance, but getting closer.

"What is it?" Roan asked.

"I hear him, or someone. I hear footsteps coming this way," Amelia said, pulling herself to her feet. Roan did the same, stretching and yawning. They both stepped cautiously out into the fading light.

"Everyone's gone," Ambrose said to them both as he came around the corner, then glanced at Roan, "How did you do today?"

"She did it. I didn't turn all day. From what we understand so far, this could be a temporary influence. Something that would need to be done each morning. But it *is* possible," Roan explained.

"Your father is expecting us to have a final meeting tonight, so we should get going. We'll meet him at the den. By the time we make it, it should be nightfall, or close enough," Ambrose said, taking off without another word.

Amelia reached out to grab Roan's hand this time, both of them following Ambrose across the open countryside.

While they walked, she thought.

She didn't want to go back to the city alone. And if today was a success, she dared to think that every day could be the same, with a little effort. But that meant getting Anatole to agree to let Roan leave the pack. At least temporarily anyhow.

Roan had been so supportive during her adjustment after the Unbinding that she almost looked at him as a guide. She felt like she needed him. That they were friends now and maybe a little more. Which was a good place to start for now. She didn't want him to stay behind. She knew it was selfish of her, but she couldn't help the way she felt.

She wasn't sure how all of it would go, but she was willing to try and persuade Anatole. Being so truly unique and different from anyone else, she felt lonely without Roan. And if she had any questions about her Larougo side, or if anything came up that she needed help with, she knew he would be there for her. Somehow, she knew that she could count on him.

Building a house out here was still an option, and one that Ambrose had already agreed to, but she would much rather have other options as well. And from the way Roan talked, so would he. They'd need to work out all the specifics, but first things first. Anatole.

As Ambrose predicted, the night was closing in as they heard the yips of dingos in the distance, turning one by one to human voices.

Amelia's sensitive eyesight had seen his form coming toward them, long before anyone else had. As he drew near enough for Ambrose to see, he greeted him with seriousness. "Anatole, good morning."

"Ah Ambrose, good morning. And welcome back Amelia, it's so nice to see the Unbinding was a success, and that you and Roan are getting on well together." His teeth flashed white against the growing darkness as he smiled.

"Can we speak in private?" Ambrose asked his fellow leader.

"Of course, please come inside," he said leading them all the short distance to the den entrance. Amelia smiled thinking of Ambrose crawling his way into the den, but then again, he must have been here before at some point, she reasoned.

As they entered the den, Anatole took the same corridor to the room he and Amelia had spoken in days before, when he first put forth his proposal to her. Having four people in the small space was difficult. Anatole and Ambrose took the chairs at the small desk, while Roan sat on the bed, motioning for her to do the same.

"First, I want to say thank you for allowing Roan to stay with Amelia. He's been a great comfort to her, while she was in isolation," Ambrose said, starting the conversation in a friendly tone.

"And how is our Amelia?" Anatole said, looking at her carefully, making her feel like she was being put on the spot.

"Fine. Great," she answered him, keeping her replies short and concise.

"Any concerns with the Unbinding? Did you transition during the day?"

"No, I didn't. The same sensitivity to light, although Roan and I discovered, if I can endure the brightness, my eyes will adapt in a similar way as my skin. I still have difficulty with loud noises. But it's not as bad as it was when I first Unbound," she said, trying to present her answer in a Roan-like clinical way.

"She's doing fine, Anatole. More than fine. Her mind is strong, she's able to control both sides of her new self. I don't think she's a danger at all. In fact, I'm proposing to allow her and Roan to come back to the city with me tonight." Pride snuck through Ambrose's wall, as he looked over at his granddaughter.

"And how would that be possible, during the day? Roan can't be inside or run freely through the streets of Perth during the day. It's too dangerous, I can't allow your request," Anatole said resolutely.

"Amelia can influence me, father. She did it this morning. I didn't transition," he said. Leaving Anatole to stare. Finally, at a loss for words. "We understand that her influence has its limits. That we may have to repeat the same routine each day. But I'm agreeable, as long as she is," Roan continued.

"You can influence my son. Have you tried with anyone else?" Anatole said leaning over toward her.

"No," she answered flatly.

"I asked her to try, I trust her. She wasn't entirely comfortable at first, but we see now that it was a success," Roan said as he looked at Amelia.

Anatole stayed deep in thought as Roan reached out and grabbed Amelia's hand, reassuring her that he was there.

"You did not change during the day?" Anatole asked Amelia again.

"No, I didn't. Not fully, I did have some change. Most noticeably my nails and teeth," she admitted. She wasn't outright lying. She was just leaving out the immunity part.

"Can you be more specific?" Ambrose was the one who was curious now.

"My normal human teeth grew, only longer and sharper. My nails did the same. But that was the extent of my changing," she said, again being very clinical and selective with her words.

"I witnessed it myself today. Just as she described," Roan backed her up.

"Were you aware of this Ambrose?" Anatole asked.

"I was not, although it's not to be unexpected. Some changes during the day," he said dismissing Anatole's pointed question. "She was in isolation during her first day, no one was allowed to visit, not knowing what to expect."

"And you trusted her, to influence you, Roan?" Anatole looked back to this son.

"I did. I do. She's been honest with me, and I feel that she's a trustworthy woman. Yes, I trust her."

Amelia smiled at him, a silent thank you. She turned back to Ambrose and Anatole. "When we first talked, you had said that this would, or could all happen. You've been proven correct," she chose her words carefully, making her case. "The 'experiment', also known as me, was a success. I've proven that I am no threat to either Larougo, or Garkain."

Amelia squeezed Roan's hand gently. "Roan can affirm that my time after the Unbinding was difficult, but that over the past two days, we've learned together how to overcome some of the challenges and work as a team. If, as you believe, our children inherit my same dual genetics, your plan will have succeeded," she finished her pitch, feeling like she'd just led a meeting at work

"You're very well-spoken when you want something," Anatole said.

"I'm going to choose to take that as a compliment," Amelia shot back, attempting to continue to exude confidence.

"There's only one part you're leaving out," Anatole noted.

"The Larougo venom. Does it affect you?" he said, meeting her eyes and holding her, while her gaze never wavered, never left his.

"I wouldn't know. At least not yet. Roan didn't transition this morning, and I haven't been infected," she lied as convincingly as she could.

"For now, that's an unknown. But all of the things we do know about Amelia, about her gift, and her differing traits, were things we always suspected or assumed. This means that the idea of bringing her home, bringing her here, the Unbinding, was all a success," Roan jumped in, deflecting the conversation as well.

"If it's true, as you say it is, that you can influence my son, not to turn. Would you be able to use your gift on other Larougo as well?" Anatole asked.

"I've been locked in a room for two days, with only Roan. I don't know the answer to your question. It's possible, but I wouldn't know," she answered honestly.

"She didn't want to at first, as I said. She didn't like the idea of it. But I insisted. We've all hated the change. It was my chance to see if there was a way around it. She took some convincing, but it worked. And it lasted all day," Roan said.

"I think the only reason it worked is that we have a connection. Roan was willing to let me into his thoughts. If he had resisted, it may not have worked. With someone I don't know well, or that isn't willing, I doubt I would be able to. Or that it wouldn't have the same long-lasting effects on them.

"When I was human, my mother influenced me several times, and each time it wore off. I fought my way out of it. It wasn't permanent. She assumed that my Larougo side played a role in that. If Roan tried to fight through my influence, he may have turned," Amelia explained.

"Have you tried to influence any member of the Colony?" Ambrose jumped in.

"No. As I've already said, you've had me isolated for two days. I haven't had the opportunity to see anyone but Roan, and you. And mother has already told me that influencing other Garkain is against the rules of the Colony. I wouldn't have tried," she said.

The two elders asked for privacy. Amelia and Roan made their way back into the main den. The chatter around them made it impossible for her to focus in on Ambrose and Anatole's private conversation. She wished she knew what they were talking about.

"Are you nervous?" she asked Roan.

"A little, you?"

Amelia nodded but tried to be polite, as so many Larougo came up and welcomed her as an honorary member of the pack. It was strange to feel a part of two societies, two worlds that she represented equally. She'd never thought of herself as part of the pack, but now she realized that's exactly how she was being treated.

"Everyone in the pack likes you," Roan teased, trying to get her to smile.

"Everyone here is curious, that's all," she said.

"Not true. You do realize that you have two families now. Right?"

"I was just thinking that. Maybe it's you who can read my emotions," she smiled at him.

"Maybe it's a bit of both," he said, daring to steal a kiss.

Anatole cleared his throat, cutting into their moment. She may be a part of two families but dealing with two different leaders might be tougher than she thought.

"We've reached a decision," Anatole said, motioning for Roan and Amelia to follow him back to the room.

SAYING GOODBYE

Amelia tried to get a read on Anatole's emotions, but the main one she was able to tap into was sadness. She didn't know what that meant, and she was more than a little nervous.

Ambrose was still at his same spot in the chair, turning as they came back into the room.

"Your grandfather and I have spoken. We've disagreed and agreed on things. But we have come to an agreement. We hope you will both be agreeable as well," Anatole spoke first, then allowed Ambrose to take the floor.

"Amelia, your abilities, and your traits are unique. If used without consideration or restraint, you could prove dangerous. However, you've also proven that you can be trusted and that you've been able to control yourself after what I can say, is the most surprising Unbinding ritual I've witnessed.

"Firstly, Amelia must agree to never use her gift without the consent of the other party. Either Garkain or

Larougo. The punishment for doing so would be decided among a joint council of both groups. You are now bound by the laws and rules of both our societies, and accountable to them.

"Secondly, in fulfillment of your previous agreement made with Anatole, you and Roan are to complete the joining ritual, which will secure your union as mates, by the year's end. Which would be six months from now."

Amelia looked to Roan, who nodded. "I understand, agree, and promise to use my gift only when asked, for either Garkain or Larougo. I'm also willing to complete the joining ritual," she offered. "I will request three months in which to return to the States and get my affairs in order. I also request that Roan be allowed to accompany me."

"I've already come to a decision about that, after Ambrose mentioned him leaving tonight, with you. Roan is free to make his own choices in this and any matter that concerns you both," he said looking to his son. The sadness she felt earlier flourished inside him. He was sad, Amelia realized, over the possibility of losing his son.

"The final condition is a sensitive one, so allow me to be blunt," Ambrose warned. "Amelia will attempt to conceive a child. To see if, being part Garkain, the passing on of your combined genetics is even a possibility. The whole reason for bringing you back to the Colony and the deal you made with Anatole was to continue your combined bloodline."

"I understand," Amelia answered, as she considered the negotiations she would like to propose. "I request to be given one year after the joining ritual as a time limit. A total of one and a half years to come to a reasonable conclusion on the possibility of our ability to conceive a family."

"A reasonable request," Ambrose weighed in.

"I agree, one and a half years," Anatole seconded.

"Roan, we can leave as soon as you'd like. But I understand if you would like some time," Ambrose offered.

"Could I have an hour?" he asked as Amelia felt his nervous energy. He was excited and also sad. Whatever differences he and his father had dealt with in the past, it didn't change the fact that they were sad to say goodbye.

"Of course, Amelia and I will wait outside," Ambrose offered as Roan nodded.

Amelia followed Ambrose through the main hall and out of the tunnel, standing in the darkness and the cool air.

"He's sad, I can tell," she confided in Ambrose when they were alone.

"He's choosing to be with you over being with his pack. He's choosing the same path your father did for your mother. It's a chance for the same situation to end much differently. He understands that, and so does Anatole. And so do I," he said letting the feeling of caring leak through his wall.

"I know you think I'm gruff and harsh. And you haven't gotten to spend a lot of time with me, outside of an official capacity. But you are my granddaughter, and I do care about what happens. About your happiness, and your safety.

"I did my best, your mother and I both did, to stop you from being sent away. We nearly broke a truce that had been hundreds of years strong, for you. I know you've felt conflicted, over whether or not you were wanted and why you were sent away. Amelia, please know this, you were always wanted. And I never stopped thinking about you every day, for twenty-five years."

Amelia felt the tears coming and she let them fall freely, as Ambrose pulled her in gently, hugging his granddaughter for the first time.

"And I am so proud of the brave, selfless, and damn near heroic girl. No, woman, that you've become."

"Thank you, grandpa," she said as the tears continued. All of her life spent wondering, and now she knew. "I won't let you down," she promised.

"I know you won't my darling girl," he said proudly. Amelia could feel his happiness as a bit of the wall completely broke free.

A shifting of dirt intruded on the quiet of the night. Both Roan and Anatole emerging from the den. Apparently, he and his father had finished saying their goodbyes.

"I'm ready when you are, love," he said as he slung the giant duffle over his shoulder with ease. It was the first time he'd used any term of endearment with her. She liked it.

Anatole and Ambrose faced each other once more, bowing and then shaking hands. Some tension had been lifted between them. Amelia could feel it. There was a sense of relief from both of them.

"Take care of my son Amelia," Anatole told her.

"I will sir," she promised.

One final hug between father and son and the three of them set off walking toward the plane on the tarmac that would take them back to Perth. Back to the hotel, back to civilization.

"I'm so nervous. Do you know that it's been over six years since I've been to the city?" Roan was beside himself with excitement.

"As long as Amelia can help you control your form through influencing, you shouldn't have any problem taking in the sights, enjoying your time together before next week," Ambrose said.

"When is your flight back to the States?" Roan asked excitedly.

"It's on the 17th, which should be what, four days from today?" she asked Ambrose.

"Exactly four days from tomorrow," he answered. "Oh, and this is for you," he said handing over a black credit card. "It's in your name, paid for by the Colony. For expenses. And we'll make sure to book an extra seat next to yours for Roan when we get back."

She didn't care that Ambrose was sitting across from them, she reached out grabbing Roan's hand, as they looked at each other smiling.

"You might find that I'm a little overwhelmed when we get back to civilization, I'm sorry to say. Even when we visited the city occasionally as children, our trips were few and far between. You're going to have to help me blend in a little," Roan said to Amelia.

"No problem," she said, shooting him a reassuring smile.

"I mean, I'm not completely clueless. But living underground, in the middle of nowhere for your entire life? My social skills are lacking, I can admit."

"You'll do fine," she said as she squeezed his hand.

The rest of the short flight was mostly filled with silence, as the six long days of the Celebration and the Unbinding rituals took their toll. Everyone was tired.

The limo was waiting as they took the steps down from the plane. Amelia never thought she would be so happy to see the city lights of Perth in the distance. She was already looking forward to a bath and a proper bed.

When they got back to the hotel they stepped from the limo, leaving Ambrose alone inside. "Oh, one more thing Amelia," he called after them. She ducked back inside, taking two boxes from his hands. Two brand new phones. "They're for you both. They're already programmed and set-up. My number, Michelle's, and your mothers are all in there if you need anything. They'll be your new phones for your new life," he said smiling.

"Thank you again, grandpa, for everything," Amelia said, giving him one last hug before stepping back out and closing the door behind her.

The night clerks at the front desk barely looked up as the couple passed on their way to the elevator bank. She scanned the key that she'd tucked into her bag before the Celebration.

"Whoa," Roan said with wide eyes, as the hotel door opened into the spacious suite. "So much better than the den," he said dropping their luggage on the floor just inside.

He picked her up and hugged her tightly, his lips brushing up against hers.

They held each other for a few minutes before Amelia pulled away. She was tired and dreadfully dirty.

"Oh my gosh I need a bath," she said with a laugh. "I stink!"

"And so do I, I'm sure," he said laughing along with her.

"No, I just mean, a full week out in the Colony with no showers, by the way. I could really use a nice hot bath. And so could my feet," she smiled.

"Ladies first! I'll see if I can't figure out the TV, something I haven't seen in a while," he said, winking at her while she slowly backed into the bathroom, closing the sliding frosted door.

She grabbed a pair of new everything from the closet and her flip flops for comfort, then ran a bath, complete with bubbles and some kind of salts from the counter by the sink. The water felt barely hot, although the steam rising from the surface told her it was.

She remembered her mother saying that Garkain barely felt hot or cold, and she marked that down as one of the things she'd miss about being human.

She carefully scrubbed herself clean, her feet, her arms, the dirt from under her chin. Stepping out, she felt nearly squeaky. Putting on clean clothes was heavenly, and her feet felt so free in her ragged old flip flops.

She wiped down the sink and the bathtub, tossing the towel in the hamper, then rolled back the door and stepped into the front room.

Roan's head turned in her direction as she came out of the bathroom. "Wow, you look . . ." he paused. Lost in how to continue. But Amelia could feel something she hadn't felt from him yet. Desire. "Clean, you look really clean," he said laughing off the embarrassment.

"It's all yours if you want to get clean, really clean too." She shot him a smirk.

He jumped up from the couch making his way toward her. "Don't mind if I do," he said stripping off his shirt as he walked past her and into the bathroom. After a few minutes she could hear the shower running.

She decided to turn off most of the lights in the front rooms, the kitchen, and the bedroom, leaving the dim light of the lamp on in the living room.

Her eyes still felt more comfortable in the low light. But the glare from the bathroom was bright. She looked toward the door, then quickly back, holding her hands over her eyes. The bright light in the bathroom, with the low light in the living room, showed the clear silhouette of a naked Roan, stripping off the rest of his clothes as he stepped into the shower.

She tried to focus on the TV, but her mind wouldn't give up the freeze-frame picture of Roan's naked silhouette. And then he started to sing. Something old, crooning under the water. Her heart raced as the water shut off, and the door opened just a crack.

"Amelia?" he called.

"Hmmm, Yeah?"

"Can you, I mean, would you mind bringing me my bag? I left it by the front door. I'm sorry," he said.

174

"Sure, no problem," she said, picking up the bag and bringing it to the door, which was still cracked. She tried not to stare, as she set the bag down just outside the door. She quickly turned back to the living room, hearing the door open all the way, and Roan dropping the heavy bag onto the tile floor.

Several minutes later and he emerged in new clothes. Nice clothes. If she had to guess, her mother's doing. While she and Ambrose stayed behind, her mother must have made sure that Roan's clothing was taken care of, expecting him to return with Amelia. Or perhaps Ambrose had let her know just before they left for the short flight back to the city.

"You look nice. You didn't happen to find those in the closet, did you?" he smiled in response. "That would be my mother's doing. I didn't even notice them when I was in there."

"She was trying to be funny, she put the bag in the shower with a note. Along with a fresh set of toiletries and body wash, which is new to me, I'm afraid to admit. But it smelled nice. The only thing she forgot was underwear," he smirked.

"And what did the note say?" Amelia asked, her curiosity piqued.

"Enjoy your new life," he smiled.

"That's kind of sweet. Would you mind if I called her and Michelle? Let them know we made it back?" she asked.

"No, not at all. I'm going to pull the couch out and get it made up while you do that. It's time to get my new schedule figured out," he said.

"Oh, you don't have to, I mean, you can sleep in the bed, if you want. Or, I can have them bring one up," Amelia said, thinking of how her mother didn't seem to like the couch much.

"No, I'll be fine here, and I don't want to keep you awake. I might have a little trouble switching my nights and days around," he said, but Amelia could feel his hesitancy at not wanting to jump right into the bed with her. She also felt respected.

"Okay, oh, I can help you with that too, if you want. My first night here was tough, but my mother helped me relax with the influencing thing," she offered.

"No offense, but maybe we shouldn't play with that too much. Just the serious stuff. Speaking of which, I'll need to set my alarm so you can, you know, before the sun comes up. I don't want to know the kind of damage I could do in a nice room like this," he said.

"That's true."

She turned back to the bedroom, sitting in one of the large chairs by the window. The last time she was here seemed like months ago, not just six days. How much your life can change, how much *her* life had changed, in such a short time was nearly incomprehensible.

She opened the new phone, tapping the icon at the bottom. Her list of favorites was already set up, as promised. Roan was first, followed by her mother, then Ambrose, and finally, Michelle.

She tapped Michelle's name and almost instantly she picked up. "Hey, you!" Her energetic voice came through the phone. "How did it go? I want to know everything!"

"I don't have the time to tell you *everything*, I just wanted to let you know that Roan and I are back at the hotel, safe and sound."

"Oh my God, you and Roan, how is that possible? Isn't he going to, you know, change once the sun comes up? You're not going to lock him in the bathroom, are you?" she joked.

"No, no. It turns out that Anatole was right, or Ambrose was. I can influence him. He doesn't have to turn. We tried it this morning, and he stayed in his human form for the entire day," Amelia explained.

"So, four full days in a posh penthouse suite, whatever will you do?" her sister said in a sly tone.

"Haha, get your mind out of the gutter. It's not like that. Yet. But we did agree to the joining ritual in six months, and one other small thing," Amelia said whispering.

"Okay, I'm all ears."

"We have to *expand* our bloodline by a year and a half from now," she said gently, hoping Michelle would get the hint.

"Holy crap! You're going to have kids! Amelia that's amazing, beyond amazing. And you're good with this, right? I mean Ambrose or Anatole didn't pressure you or anything."

"No, they didn't. It was clear when I accepted Anatole's proposal that we would, well try. And I set the timeline," she said.

"Wow, I'm in shock. I'm seriously in shock," her sister said in near hysterics.

"I think Roan and I are going to try and get out of the hotel tomorrow. He hasn't been to the city for a long time, and I need to buy a new pair of sunglasses. This light sensitivity thing is a real pain. So, I was going to ask what your plans were tomorrow. If you maybe wanted to join us for coffee, or do a little shopping?"

"I don't want to intrude on your day. But if Roan's fine with it, then yes, absolutely. It's a date. And I know all the best places to shop, believe me. Having our mother as a self-affirmed fashionista has had me in almost every shop from here to Brisbane."

"I'm sure he wouldn't mind a bit. I just hated being away from you for so long. I need to see my sister," Amelia said.

"Me too."

"I'll call you in the morning then," Amelia said, hanging up and pressing her mother's name next. This time it took a few rings before she heard her voice.

"Amelia, darling, how are you? Ambrose said that you and Roan made it back to the hotel safely. I left him some clothes and toiletries in the shower, in case he hasn't found them yet," she said.

"He did, and he says, 'thank you', and so do I. That was very thoughtful."

"Well of course! What do you two have on the agenda for tomorrow? Your first day back in town?" she asked. Amelia felt guilty telling her she'd already made plans with Michelle, but if her mother's feelings were hurt, they could make a date for another day.

"We're meeting Michelle, and grabbing coffee, maybe doing a bit of shopping in town," she said, waiting to hear her mother's response.

"That sounds wonderful, darling. Make sure to use the card Ambrose gave you. And maybe we can all get together before you leave. I have to tell my girl goodbye," her mother said.

"I'll be back, but yes, we will all hit the town together. It sounds like a plan to me," she said.

"And to me. Well, enjoy your night, and get some rest. I'll see you soon, darling. And I want you to know that I am so happy you're home. I'm proud of you, Amelia."

"Thank you," Amelia said, feelings welling up inside. "I'll give you a call tomorrow ok?"

"That sounds great, I'll talk to you then."

Hanging up with her mother she looked over to the couch. Roan had already dozed off, with the TV still on, but the sound off. She'd tell him about their date with Michelle in the morning.

She pulled back the sheets and the comforter, slipping off her flip flops and crawling into the bed she'd missed for a week straight. As soon as her head hit the down pillow, she was out.

A LEARNING CURVE

The alarm that Roan had set, sounded loudly in the quiet room, startling her awake. Amelia looked at her own phone by the bed. There was an hour before sunrise. Plenty of time to sneak into the bathroom, brush her teeth, and throw on a little bit of makeup.

She tiptoed past Roan, still fully asleep, as she hit the snooze button on his phone. Sneaking into the bathroom, she made sure she was presentable. After coming back into the room, she took the liberty of ordering breakfast, for both herself and Roan. As she hung up the phone, she heard him shifting, and sitting.

"Good morning," she said. "By the sounds of your snoring, I'd say you slept pretty good," Amelia grinned.

"I didn't keep you awake did I? I had a bit of trouble getting comfortable but then I must have just passed out from exhaustion. I may take you up on your offer tonight. For the extra bed in the room, I mean."

"No, you didn't keep me up. I can sleep through almost anything. And I'll take care of the extra bed when breakfast gets here," she said.

"When do you want to do the influencing thing?" he asked.

"That's entirely up to you. Looking at the time, I would say we have a little less than an hour before the sun comes up."

"Well, we can go ahead now, get it over with," he suggested.

"That works for me," she said, coming to sit down on the pull out bed beside him. She repeated the same process, digging deeper and deeper until she found the feeling. It was easier to find this time, she noticed, now that she knew where to look. Which was good, less time messing around inside his mind made her more comfortable.

This time he came out of the trance a lot quicker too. Maybe the less time she spent there, the less time it took for him to come back.

"And . . ." Amelia waited.

"And I feel fine, the same as yesterday. And no headache this time," he said smiling.

"You let me in a little easier today, and I knew which feeling I was looking for, so it took a lot less time," Amelia explained, as a knock came at the door.

"Oh, and I ordered our breakfast," she said with a grin.

"I'm guessing food for me and room service for you."

"Yup," she smiled.

He got up from his bed, opening the door to a rolling cart full of food. "I didn't know what you liked for breakfast, so I ordered a little of everything," Amelia said with a smirk.

"I'll eat pretty much anything, but this is perfect," he said. "And I'll leave you two alone," he whispered, taking off to the bathroom himself.

"Good morning Miss, where would you like your breakfast?" The nice young woman asked politely, as Amelia's mouth began to burn, the taste of her own blood hitting her tongue as her teeth broke through.

She stepped in front of the woman, reaching into her mind as quickly as she could. She influenced the woman that she wouldn't feel afraid. That she wanted to block out any memory of being in this room, and that she wanted to be quiet and still.

Amelia prayed it worked as she gently grabbed the woman's arm, her Garkain fangs rupturing through the woman's soft skin like butter. She barely punctured the vein in her wrist, tasting her blood. She had to control herself, to take just enough to lose the pangs of hunger. A few more big gulps and Amelia withdrew her mouth completely.

The young woman stood there, unmoving as Amelia watched the coagulant in her saliva stop the flow of blood. Two small and barely noticeable marks colored her skin, but the wound was sealing over already.

"Thank you for breakfast," Amelia said, hoping the woman would take her cue and leave. But she still stood silent, unmoving.

Amelia re-thought what she had influenced the girl to do. Ah, be quiet and be still. She very well might stay quiet and still all day. Shit, she thought.

"Uh oh, what did you do?" Roan said, laughing as he came out of the bathroom.

"Oh, hush! I told her she felt like being quiet and still. Now she won't speak or move," Amelia said with frustration, as Roan erupted in laughter. "And you are not helping! Shh, I need to concentrate."

"Okay," Roan silently laughed in the background as Amelia felt her way back into the woman's mind. She influenced her to feel like it was time to go about her normal day, and that the couple in the penthouse was very nice to her.

"If there's anything at all I can do, just let me know Miss," The woman said, coming out of it.

"Wait, yes, there is. I almost forgot. We're going to need another bed in here," Amelia told her.

"I can bring in a rollaway, if you'd like," The woman offered.

"No, I mean like a real bed, frame, mattress, and all," Amelia re-phrased.

"I'm sorry Miss, we can't do that," the woman said apologetically.

Amelia sighed. "The rollaway will be fine, thank you."

"Yes Ma'am, I'll have one sent right up."

She watched as the woman rolled the table away. Roan had already cleared it while Amelia was trying to fix her mistake. The entire breakfast menu was laid out on the table as Roan sat, taking his plate and piling it high.

"Didn't go as planned did it?" Roan said with a snide smile.

"Hey, it's not as easy as it looks, and that was my first time, with the whole feeding thing. With you, I know exactly where I'm going, and what I'm looking for now. I know what the end result is supposed to be. But trying to convince someone they're okay with a stranger nibbling on their arm is a little new."

Roan started laughing again. "Hey, I was going to go back in and influence her to bring a real bed in here, but I didn't want to scramble the poor girl's brain," Amelia said, as she burst into laughter too.

"So, I didn't mention is last night, because by the time I got off the phone you were nodding off, but Michelle and I made plans for today. And I want you to come with us. I hope that's ok," she said.

"Totally fine with me. As I said, it's been ages since I've been to the city, and I'd like to look around. And I like your sister, she seems nice. A little ditsy, but nice. I know she cares about you. And since we're all going to be family now, I'd better get to know them all a little better," he grinned.

"Then I will leave you to your breakfast, while I get changed into something more comfortable, as in sneakers," Amelia said trotting off to the bathroom and closing the door to the closet. Jeans and a light gauzy purple sweater seemed right. She dug through her original suitcase finding her comfy pink and white sneakers, pulling them on too.

"All set," she said as she walked back into the kitchen.

"And I am stuffed. Thank you again for the breakfast. Now I'm going to change and then we can get out of this room!"

"I'll text Michelle and see when she wants to meet us," she called after him. Michelle texted back right away, as Amelia figured she would, offering to meet them whenever they were ready. She was already here, which didn't surprise Amelia at all. Michelle seemed to be early to everything.

"I'm ready, how do I look?" he asked as Amelia looked up from the phone.

Amazing, sexy, attractive, I want to kiss you. All these thoughts flew through her head in an instant. His hair falling just across his eyes, the black polo shirt fitting just perfectly to show off his muscular physique. And altogether, he looked like a model or a movie star. She suddenly felt very possessive.

"Um, good, I mean great. You look great. Perfect actually," she stumbled through her words. "You know, Michelle? Right, well she's waiting in the lobby right now, so if you're ready I'm ready," she said turning away as she squeezed her eyes shut with embarrassment.

The entire ride down to the lobby she chastised herself for acting like such a fool. She kept avoiding eye contact as much as she could. Thank God he couldn't read *her* emotions, she thought.

The door opened into the main lobby, as two lattes were thrust in both their faces. "Coffee?" Michelle offered.

"Yes, please, but I think you've reached your limit," Amelia quipped, as she reached out hugging her sister tightly. "It's so good to see you, you have no idea," Amelia whispered.

"You too," Michelle said finally letting go.

"And I'm glad I finally get some time with you, brother-in-law, kind of," Michelle said laughing to herself.

"She's not usually this crazy, I promise. Actually no, I don't promise," she said to Roan, loudly so her sister could hear.

"Okay, point taken," she said, taking a deep breath. "And I'm calm now."

"Thank God. So where to first? You are our official tour guide today, just make sure we swing by somewhere close for a dark pair of glasses. My eyes will be killing me in the sun," Amelia reminded her sister.

"Right, I know just the place, but first, we need to acclimate," she said with a sigh.

"Roan, we need to stay in the sun for a minute or two before we head out if you want to be our cover. Mother stood just off to the left of the back door, there's a semi-private area there, where we can wait."

"Perfect! I had to rush to the bathroom and hang out in a stall. That's where I was when you texted, by the way, before I got coffee," Michelle said, as the group headed out of the back door of the lobby.

Her transition was quicker than Michelle's she noticed, as less than a few minutes passed and she was a deep golden brown. She waited patiently for Michelle to achieve the same dark tan, and then the three of them set off on their adventure through the city.

"Tell me about you Roan. Leave nothing out, I must know everything!" Michelle said as they walked past by the Marina enjoying the cloudless sky.

"Not much to tell really. I've been a part of the pack since birth obviously, and I spend most of my time with them. This whole life is completely foreign to me, so take it easy on my first day in the real world," he said. "I have two degrees, online courses. I'm kind and understanding, and I think I kind of really like your sister," he shot Amelia a wink.

"I'm sold," Michelle said, then turned her attention to Amelia. "So, what's it like, being half Larougo and half Garkain? I only saw you once after you Unbound, what's it been like since then?"

"Challenging, but exciting. My eyes are doing better with the whole adjusting thing, but it's still tough. My hearing is a lot better. I can focus on things, but it's not the overwhelming noise like it was in the beginning.

"I can feel everyone's, well almost everyone's emotions very strongly. You nearly knocked me out with yours this morning, by the way. And I think I'm getting the hang of the gift. This morning I had breakfast, and with one minor hiccup, everything went fine." She could hear Roan chuckling in the background.

"Oh, you hush," Amelia said jokingly.

"What's so funny?" Michelle asked, glancing from Roan to Amelia.

"She told the poor girl to be quiet and still, then she couldn't get her to leave," he told Michelle still laughing.

"Look, it was my first time, other than you. But I fixed it. She did leave. Eventually," she told Michelle, who was still grinning from ear to ear.

"Don't feel bad. Mother had to help me with my first influence, and it didn't go that great either. I couldn't get into the guy's mind quick enough, and then he started asking me why I was staring at him," Michelle admitted. "I think he thought I was trying to get his number or something."

"Okay, that's almost as bad as mine!" Amelia said, not feeling quite as embarrassed.

"Shut up," Michelle said nudging her sister into Roan's side, which he happily took as an opportunity to throw his arm around her.

"It does seem like you two are getting along well, I'm happy for you. Both of you," Michelle said.

They followed Michelle around and around, through different parts of town that Amelia hadn't been to yet. She noticed that the shops began to look much fancier as they kept walking.

"Okay, so, quick cheat. Before you go into a store, stand in the shade, and let your skin change, obviously. An alleyway, like that one there will work just fine. Keep your head down and look at your phone, no one likes to bother people who appear busy," Michelle instructed.

The girls did exactly that, while Roan stood at the entrance to the narrow alley looking bored but not complaining. A few minutes later, and noticeably paler, they walked into one of the high-end stores, one specifically selling sunglasses in every tint and style, color, and shape Amelia could imagine.

She tried on each pair, but every time she looked toward the window and the glare from the sun, they were never quite dark enough. Finally, she found a pair that worked.

"Holy shit," she said as she looked at the price tag.

"Well, you have good taste. Designer taste. I guess that runs in our genes too," Michelle said with a laugh. "What do you think that card Ambrose gave you is for anyway?"

"Are you sure?" Amelia said with a flash of shock.

"Absolutely," Michelle said nodding. "And they look great on you."

They paid for the expensive glasses, then took their time staying in the shade and browsing from store to store. Amelia picked out a few more things that she liked and even convinced Roan to pick a few things for himself.

She doubted this was the kind of day he had in mind, but he was a good sport, which she greatly appreciated. She'd make it up to him.

She felt like he'd put up with enough shopping for one day, so they decided to go to the park and walk around for a while there. It was a pain to have to acclimate every time she walked into and out of a place. Another thing she marked down as a con.

By early afternoon, Amelia suggested they stop by one of the food trucks near the park, so Roan could grab something to eat.

"Eating in front of you two isn't fair when I know you've got to be hungry too. I'll wait here while you two grab something, or someone for yourselves," he said, taking a huge bite of his burger.

"Sounds good to me, I saw a small dive with only a few people inside just back over that way, we can grab something in there," Michelle suggested.

"Okay, we'll be right back," Amelia said to Roan.

"I'm not worried at all. I'm sure you two will be just fine," he smiled.

At the small restaurant, the two wandered inside. The light dim enough to hide their skin transition. As Michelle had said, there were a handful of patrons inside taking lunch at this hour. A couple at a table near the back caught Amelia's attention.

Michelle whispered, "Okay, so we'll tell them they need to go to the bathroom, and that they want to follow us. Then tell them that they want us to feed on them and that they don't want to make a sound while in the room. That should work, I hope."

She nudged Michelle and gestured in their direction. Michelle nodded, and they headed for the table. Michelle took the lead.

"Hey guys," she said in a friendly tone to the couple. Who looked confused, but returned her hello, not wanting to appear rude.

The two women quickly sat. Amelia taking the woman, and Michelle taking the man. They both stared at their person, delving quickly into their minds. As the women both stood, the couple followed them into one of the restrooms. The rest was quick.

Amelia rinsed her mouth in the sink, while Michelle did the same after her. The two women walked out of the dimly lit joint as easily as they walked in, and far less hungry.

Returning to the park they spotted Roan, sitting just where they left him.

"Better?" he asked. The girls both nodded, as he stood. "So, what's next?" Roan asked.

"How about we just walk around for a bit, take a swing by the Marina on the way back to the hotel," Michelle suggested.

"Sounds good," Roan said, although Amelia knew he'd had about enough for the day, and so had she, honestly.

Michelle sensed her sister's mood, being kind enough to end their outing. "Well, I think I've had it for today, and I can honestly say that you, my dear sister, got lucky," she said, shooting her a smile.

"And you better live up to the high opinion I already have of you," Michelle said, looking Roan right in the eyes.

"I promise, to not only meet, but exceed your expectations," he said with a playful bow.

They said their goodbye's and the pair snuck back in through the rear door, heading quickly to the elevator before Amelia's skin began to change.

Back in the suite, she landed face-first onto the bed, dropping their bags next to it.

"Ugh, what a day! But a good day?" she said with a hint of a question.

GIVING IN OR STANDING UP

The next morning the couple repeated their routine. Breakfast for them both and influencing Roan to stay human throughout the day. It was slowly becoming their new normal.

With a full day ahead of them and no plans to speak of, they sat and drank coffee all morning. Eventually having to order another pot, as the gray day outside the window made the hotel room seem warm and cozy.

Clouds had moved in overnight, bathing the view of the marina below in a gray light. By late morning, the first rumbles of thunder had started, and drops of rain appeared on the wall of windows by the bed. It was the perfect day to do nothing, staying inside and talking. It felt comfortable. Nice.

"So you live where again?" Roan asked her.

"I live just North of Houston in a small town called Woodhills, it's nice. I saved for years to buy the house I live in. There's a mall and lots of walking trails. I lived with a foster family there when I was younger and when I grew up, I knew that's where I wanted to live.

"My adopted family lives in Houston, about forty-five minutes away. We don't see each other that much. Mainly for holidays or birthdays. Obligation stuff mostly."

"I've always heard about Christmas and Thanksgiving, truly American holidays. What's it like to grow up in America?" he kept asking question after question, excitement flowing from him as they talked.

"Christmas is huge. Stores begin putting out decorations and Christmas themed items months before December. Thanksgiving has always been a time to over-indulge in food, fall asleep while watching football on TV. Don't Larougo have any holidays or traditions?" she asked.

"Not really. In the same way that the Garkain only have the Celebration twice a year. We don't have holidays. Rituals, and gatherings yes, but no set days or traditions. Both our kinds are different, we don't exactly fit into the normal society. So, holidays are kind of a human thing.

"I know that in the city they celebrate those things. Especially Christmas. I've heard stories, but I've never seen it. I'd like to though," he said.

"We will. It's July now, so we'll actually be getting . . . joined, I guess, in December sometime. We'll be back in Australia by then, and we can enjoy all the lights and decorations," she smiled. Some of her best memories and her worst were during the holidays. The joyous atmosphere that time of year, mixed with the sadness of not having the family she wanted there to share it with. But this year would be different.

"And you work?"

Amelia nodded. "I'm an office manager for a doctor's office. I handle all the paperwork and the billing. It's boring at times, but I like helping people. People who are sick. I fight the insurance companies, so they can get the help they need.

"That's part of what I need to take care of. I'll have to put my notice in. Put the house up for sale. Say goodbye to the people I work with. Close up my entire life in the States."

"No friends? No boyfriend?" Roan asked. He'd been holding onto that one for a while, she thought.

Amelia chuckled. "No boyfriend. Not anymore. And I don't have many friends. A few that I talk to every once in a while, but no one close. I'm not good at getting out there and making friends. I'm kind of an introvert, I guess. The boyfriend, or ex-boyfriend, I met in college. We stayed together for a few years, but only because it was too hard to call it quits.

"And how about you? Anyone in the pack that you've dated? Wait, do you date, or have girlfriends? How *does* that work?" Amelia asked.

"Well, we do in a way. Larougo choose life mates. So, we do date, I guess. But for me it was a little different, being Anatole's son, and next in line for leadership, my 'dates' were selected. I didn't have a choice in the matter. We're a small society and not as diverse as yours. So, my options were limited. And let's say that even if given the choice myself, I couldn't find myself attracted to anyone. Living in the pack, we're all kind of family, so all the girls there I grew up with. We played together as kids."

"So you don't have any children?" Amelia asked, immediately wishing she could take the question back, as Roan started laughing loudly. "Why is that so funny?" Amelia demanded.

"It's not, it's not, I guess. It's just that you said it so worried. Dare I say jealous?" Roan teased her. "It's cute. I like it."

"I'm not jealous, I'm curious," Amelia said resolutely.

"Sorry, I'm sorry, my mistake. But no, I haven't been with anyone, if that's what you're asking. There's a kind of bond that you feel, at least within the pack. A feeling that's indescribable. It's how we know who our mate is supposed to be. I never felt it with anyone, and some never do, but good relationships are made without it," he said with a shrug.

Amelia's eyes shot wide on their own. Was she hearing this correctly? That Roan was . . . had never . . . no that couldn't be right. She had, of course. Being in a relationship for two years, of course she had. But Roan? The conversation stalled as the room had that awkward feel to it.

Thoughts flitted through her head. If he was a virgin and she wasn't, would he think less of her? Would that somehow be seen as a black mark on her within his Larougo customs?

"Roan, can I be blunt?" she asked, figuring the best way to handle this was to just go for it.

"That sounds perfect to me. And I think I might join you in that nap. Over here, I mean," he grinned.

She turned and made her way to the bed, fighting not to ask the question she wanted to so badly right now. Curling up between the comforter and the sheets, the bed suddenly felt too big.

"Roan?" she called.

"Yeah."

"Would you, I mean, if you wanted to take a nap with me in the bed, I wouldn't mind." She hoped she was being clear enough with just a bit of vagueness, so he could make his own choice.

His feet softly padded along the carpet as she felt him lay on top of the covers next to her. She smiled at how boyish he was in some ways. How nervous and inexperienced living outside of civilization had made him. She rolled over on her back, seeing him respectfully facing away from her.

She smiled and rolled over, tossing her arm around him. Feeling his frame against hers. She felt safe here and now. She felt secure and happy. She dozed for a while, enjoying the comfort of not being alone anymore.

Her phone rang later in the afternoon, her mother's name popping up on the screen. She groaned and swiped to answer. "Hello?"

"Hello, darling. I hope I didn't disturb you two," she said with a pause.

"Nope, nothing to disturb, just taking a nap. What's up?" she said not hiding the irritation in her voice.

"I wanted to see how my daughter was doing. Michelle said you three had a great day yesterday, and we'd talked about spending a day together. I was thinking about tomorrow, seeing as that's your last full day here before you leave us for a little while." Amelia felt something odd from her mother through the phone suddenly. Jealousy. Maybe she was jealous that they'd spent the day with Michelle and not her, Amelia thought.

"Tomorrow would be great, as long as Roan is up for another day out," she said.

"Sounds good to me," he mumbled from his side of the bed, obviously still dozing.

"We'll meet you in the lobby just after sunrise," Amelia told her mother.

"I'll see you then," her mother said, hanging up.

Amelia tossed the phone onto the bed, rolling back over and resuming her comfortable position. "We should get up," she groaned. "We wasted most of the day."

Roan turned to face her, his dark eyes locking onto hers. "I wouldn't say we wasted it."

"True," she agreed, forcing herself to turn away. The way he looked right now, her willpower was being tested almost to its breaking point.

She felt his fingers gently run along her back, sending chills down her spine. The tension was getting to a breaking point. Both of them resisting the inevitable, resisting their own desires and urges. Their self-control was being pushed to the limit.

Every breath was intimate in the quiet of the room. Every glance was an invitation. "Roan, we don't have to," she said as she turned toward him. Her eyes saying the exact opposite.

"Amelia, I may be inexperienced, but that doesn't mean I don't know what I want," he said as he pulled her on top of him, sliding his hands up and down her skin under her shirt.

The gentle grazing of lips on lips continued until she could no longer take it. She grabbed his face, pressing her mouth to his. Sheets and clothes littered the floor, as the sounds of passion replaced the silence.

They lay together, comfortable, and quiet. Wrapped in the sheets that managed to stay on the bed. They passed the rest of the day exchanging glances until night came.

She dreamt wildly again that night. She dreamed she was back home. She dreamed about the house in the outback, the one that she had initially intended for her and Roan to call home. And then the alarm sounded, ripping her from her dreams and her sleep.

She rolled over, carefully grabbing her shirt from between the tangled bedclothes, slipping it over her, then searching for her pajama bottoms as Roan rolled over, pulling her back into bed. "We still have time," he grumbled.

"Considering we're meeting my mother downstairs in a little over an hour, we really don't."

"Oh right, okay," he said, getting out of bed as she made sure to look the other way. "Modesty? Now?" he laughed.

"Just go get your clothes on. And yes, I'm trying to be a lady," she shot back.

"Then I will be a gentleman. I'll see you in a sec. Don't suppose we have time for breakfast?" he asked.

"We can eat downstairs in the restaurant for a change if we hurry," Amelia said, waiting for him to get dressed, so she could freshen up herself.

She bolted past Roan into the bathroom as he came out. "I'll be just a minute and then we'll be good!" she yelled as she slammed the sliding door behind her. Combing through her wild hair was a challenge, but she managed to look decent. She threw on her same jeans and the same top from the other day, then made it into the living room, just in time.

She was getting much better at influencing Roan to resist the change. It was almost like the more she modified that singular feeling, the closer to the surface it was getting, or that's how it felt. It was also easier, a simple nudge as the feeling slipped into place, like a key into a lock.

"Okay, all set," she said rushing for the door.

"Wait, wait just a minute," Roan said, gently grabbing her arm and turning her to face him. "I didn't get to tell you good morning yet," he said with a deep kiss that made Amelia want to stay in the room for one more day.

"Good Morning," he said, letting her go.

"Good Morning!"

They made it down to LuLu's with just about thirty minutes to spare before her mother should be meeting them in the lobby.

The restaurant was busy, but not overly so, as their waiter showed them to their table in the corner. She texted her mother where they were, promising to be with her

Her mother didn't respond and the atmosphere inside the car became stagnant. Amelia was beyond grateful when they rolled to a stop, Trevor opening the door for them.

Inside the aquarium, miles of glass walls provided a picture into the undersea world. Thousands of fish in varying colors swam this way and that around the coral reefs. Amelia watched as Roan seemed entranced by the scenery. She couldn't help but smile, and she wished that this was their moment. That they were alone.

"It's wonderful isn't it?" her mother said, coming up beside her. "They even have a restaurant here, where you can enjoy your dinner with ambiance. You and Roan should come one night when you get back to Perth," she said.

Amelia was trying to remain calm, but all the heavy-handed hints and talk about living in the city, or worse, in the same building, was beginning to piss her off. What was this woman's deal, all of a sudden? She drew back her feelings, trying to create the same wall that Ambrose was able to achieve. She understood now why he felt the need for one.

"We'll consider it," Amelia said, intentionally careful to avoid any verbal commitments.

"Excuse me for a moment," she said to her mother, going to one of the exhibits and joining Roan.

"This is so awesome. I'm sorry, but I've studied most, if not all of these species on the internet, and getting to see them up close is amazing." He marveled at the fish through the glass.

Thank God for Roan, Amelia thought. He could make her smile, just by being himself. And right now, she couldn't imagine being without him.

She'd been feeling something new from him lately in addition to desire, not much, just a small spark, but this morning it had grown. Love. And she realized as she watched him now, at this moment, that she was beginning to feel the same. Maybe not quite love, but definitely something. More than what she originally thought there would be for sure.

She stayed close to Roan for the rest of the time they were at the aquarium, keeping the conversation light, and steering clear of any talk about the future, just to play it safe. Amelia looked at her phone. 1:00 in the afternoon.

"I'm sorry Roan," she said to both him and her mother, "but I'm starting to get a little tired. And we need to get everything sorted for tomorrow."

She could tell he was slightly disappointed, but she did make a mental note of her mother's date night suggestion. Maybe they would come back some day. She just needed to get away from her mother right now.

"I'm so sorry to hear that, darling. We were having such a great time I thought," her mother said. "But I understand, and I'll make sure that Trevor helps you to the airport in the morning."

"That would be lovely, thank you," she said to Phoebe as they headed for the exit.

The ride back was just as awkward, and she was more than sure that Roan had picked up on it too. As he sat quietly, keeping to himself.

Pulling up at the hotel was a relief as her mother insisted on following them inside the lobby. Amelia turned and hugged her, making sure that their goodbyes were said down there. Above all, she didn't want her mother trying to follow them up to their room.

"Thank you for everything, and don't worry, we'll be fine," Amelia said as she released her mother.

"I'll keep her safe. You have my word," Roan said reverently, and with a slight bow.

"I know you will. I love you, Amelia. I'm so proud of you, and I can't wait for you to be back home for good. I'll call and check in on you, and I'll be looking forward to seeing you in a few months," she said as she turned and headed for the front doors and the limo.

Inside the elevator, Roan turned to her. "What the hell was all that about?"

"I don't know. But I didn't like the way our day went. Something's not right. I can feel it. I'll tell you more in the room."

QUESTIONS

"Turn your phone off," Amelia said in a low tone, pressing the button on the side of hers, then tossing it on the bed. She motioned for Roan to follow her into the bathroom. He raised an eyebrow but turned off his phone as she asked, then walked into the bathroom behind her, closing the door.

Amelia turned on the faucets, then pulled him into the shower.

"Are you crazy?" he asked. "Because I kind of need to know now," he said with mock seriousness.

"Something's off. Something's not right. In the States, they have apps, apps that people put on phones to track and spy on people. They can listen to conversations when people don't know it. Even use location settings to track them.

"And I'm not sure the room isn't wired. I thought it was sweet that my mother had come in and brought you all new clothes, but now after today, it seems creepy. Like an intrusion on our privacy."

He stood listening, not making fun, but genuinely listening. "I'm following you, a little."

"Michelle with all the questions the other day, and then my mother pushing us to move into the same building with them? Doesn't that strike you as a little, weird?"

"Okay, yes. And I appreciate you putting her off. You know her better than I do, so I kept my mouth shut. But yeah, today was a little weird," he agreed.

"Not only that, but the feeling I got from her was *jealousy*. What the hell could she be jealous about?"

He sighed, sitting on the stone bench inside the shower. "Think about it. You're living her life for one thing. The life she was supposed to have with Lachlean is the one you get to have with me.

"Another thing is, you're powerful, not just in your abilities, but considering the fact that we're the start of something new, it won't be long before you're taking over her position of power inside the Colony. To her, you're a threat."

Amelia considered everything he was saying, and she could see his point. But it still didn't explain the possessive way she tried to convince them to move in with her and Michelle and Robert.

"I see where you're going with this, but what about the insisting that we move to the city? Trying to convince us to move into the same damn building as her? I was getting mad. It's one thing to politely suggest something, but the woman wouldn't let it go!" Amelia was getting frustrated again, she could feel it.

"That I think is a Garkain thing. In the same way we value life partners, Garkain's direct bloodlines are close. As in very close. That's one reason why the ritual is done by a direct link. And it's usually the mother. Garkain mothers are very possessive over their children, that could be a big reason. Their opinions hold a lot of weight with their offspring usually.

"Being that you're strong-willed and independent-minded, *and* that you haven't been made to understand that tradition, she might feel like you're being hard-headed. But that's all the things I love about you. You're not a follower. You're a leader, and I think that intimidates her too. Can we get out of the shower now?" he smiled.

"Yes, but we have to go run an errand," Amelia said.

She turned off all the faucets and grabbed their phones, powering them back on briefly and writing down the five numbers in their contacts, then powering them both off again.

"Let's go," Amelia said. "We're about to find out."

She remembered seeing an electronics store in one of the strip centers not far away. Heading off, she cut straight past the marina, instantly recognizing the storefront.

"Good afternoon, we need two new phones and new numbers. We're just in from the States and we need a phone and carrier that works better here," she told the clerk behind the counter.

"Not a problem at all Miss, do you know which phone you'd like to go with?" the clerk politely asked.

"The newest and the best," she said, pulling out and laying down the black card on the glass counter.

"Just a minute," the clerk said, ducking into the back storeroom.

"If I'm right about the phones then my mother will have a shit fit when I give her our new numbers. And if I'm wrong then we have two phones. But personally, I feel more comfortable having our own account and our own phones."

"Fine by me," he said. Amelia could tell he thought she was being over-paranoid, but she didn't care.

She knew about spyware, and she had a gut feeling that changing phones and numbers would have some unwelcome response from her mother.

What really worried her was Michelle. She'd thought of her as such a close friend and a true sister. She hated to think she would possibly go along with spying on the two of them. Then again, she had to remember that Michelle did go along with trying to convince her to Unbind when they had asked her to.

What really made her mad, was the kind of control her mother was trying to extend over her. And depending on her mother's reaction to the phone swap, Amelia may very well have to get Ambrose involved. She wouldn't have her life run by anyone. She never had, and never would allow someone to make her choices for her.

The clerk returned with two boxes, and a pamphlet with different carriers and plans to choose from.

"Which is the best plan for out near Ayer's Rock? We're planning on seeing the sights, renting a jeep and we don't want to be without a phone, for emergencies," Amelia explained.

"Then I would go with this one, they have the widest coverage, a bit pricier depending on the plan, but worth it if you're going off-road. You don't want to have an accident and lose reception."

"I completely agree. We'll go with the unlimited plan with the widest coverage."

"Will you be adding these phones to an established account or a new account? If you have the same carrier in the States, we could just add these two phones and numbers to it," the clerk suggested.

She did have the same carrier back home. "Can you look up my account by number?" she asked the clerk, who nodded. Amelia gave him the number, and her account popped up.

"So, I'll just add these to your current account. Will you be buying the phone's outright, or paying over time?"

"Outright," Amelia said politely. "And can you update the card on file with the new one here?" she asked.

"Absolutely. So, just give me about fifteen minutes to set up your phones and get your account updated with your new payment information, and you will be all ready to go." The clerk said with a smile.

"Fantastic, we'll just hang out for a few then," Amelia said, pointing to a long bench down one of the walls.

"Have I told you how amazing you are today?" Roan asked completely out of nowhere.

"Yes, but you can always tell me again," she said teasingly.

"You are quite simply the most amazing woman I've ever met," he said as he kissed her without hesitation.

As promised, fifteen minutes later, they were the proud owners of two new phones and numbers.

Back in the room, she grabbed the paper from the desk in the living room. She typed her mother's number into the new phone and put it on speaker. No answer.

"She doesn't recognize the number I bet," Amelia said, then saved all the numbers into the new phone and handed over the paper so Roan could do the same.

Thirty seconds later and Amelia's new phone rang. She answered, then immediately put her mother on speaker for Roan to hear.

"Hello?" Her mother's confused voice came over the line.

"Hey, it's Amelia. I wanted to give you my new number," she said in an upbeat voice. "Something was wrong with the ones that Ambrose gave us, the screens kept turning on and off," Amelia explained. Immediately she felt frustration streaming over the line as her mother paused. It was so evident that even Roan reacted, shooting her a look.

"Well darling, you should have let us know. I would have been more than happy to bring you two new ones myself," she said trying to conceal her mood by being polite.

"No problem, I have the same carrier, so I just put the new phones on my account. That way my American phone and Australian phones are on the same one." Again irritation flowed over the line as her mother held a long pause.

"Are you upset? I didn't mean to upset you," Amelia said, fishing.

"Of course not, why would I be upset?" her mother said, attempting to put Amelia on the spot.

"I know you went to all the trouble to get the new phones for us and they didn't work. You can try to return them if you'd like. I'll leave them at the front desk in the morning," Amelia offered.

"No, that's fine. If they don't work you can throw them away, or keep them, whatever you like," her mother said.

"I'll just toss them then. I'll call you once we land," Amelia said.

"Alright darling, be careful."

"I will," Amelia said and hung up, waiting for Roan to speak.

"You were right," Roan admitted. "She was definitely not happy about us switching everything over."

"You noticed it too? The feeling I got was irritation. Like she was pissed, but not outright angry. Something is up. Let's hang out in the restaurant for a bit, grab a cup of coffee. And you haven't eaten since breakfast, so I'm sure you're starving."

Roan shrugged, "I could eat."

Down in the restaurant, they continued their conversation. Away from the suite, away from their old phones.

"Let's say that you're right, that Ambrose and your mother are spying on us. The question is, why?"

"That's the answer I don't have. I guess it could be as simple as keeping tabs on us while we're back in the States. Maybe they think we're going to make a run for it. And it

"But just enough space for the pack," Amelia smiled. She saved the photo, then texted it to Ambrose, telling him this is the house she picked. He texted back: OK.

"And that is that. Ambrose originally said three months but considering the size of the house we just picked, we may have to wait a bit longer. He said 'OK'."

Back in the suite, they began to get their things together for the long plane ride tomorrow.

"Ambrose just texted me the link for our tickets, and the plane leaves at 10:00. I looked, and we should cross the international date line, which means it'll be dark when we land in Houston. Not looking forward to the jetlag," Amelia said as Roan neatly folded and packed his things.

"Perfect," he said a bit absently.

"You ok?"

"Yeah, I'm fine, just nervous, I guess."

"Hey, I've been meaning to ask you something. But I never find the right time to do it," she said, letting the sentence hang.

"Go ahead. I'll tell you anything you want to know, you know that," he answered as he stopped and turned toward her.

"Well, with everything going on between me and my family, I haven't asked that much about yours. You never talk about your mother, and I've never asked if *you* have any brothers or sisters."

Intense sadness, regret, resentment, and despair flowed from him, nearly knocking Amelia out. The feelings were so intense.

"I have a brother, older. And my mother is gone. When she left, she took him with her."

"Gone? As in . . . ?"

"No, just gone," he said with a heavy sigh. He stopped packing and came over to sit in front of her. "My father was, not a very nice man to be joined with. A good provider and a good dad overall, overbearing at times, and a lot of pressure on me and Trenton, especially Trenton. But my mother was strong, like you. She could think for herself and my father didn't like that.

"It was an arranged situation. And when she couldn't take it anymore, she made a choice. Once you're joined, there's no pack version of divorce. You just deal with it, or you leave. She left when I was a kid. Trenton was twelve, and he chose to go with her. I barely remember them," Roan said.

"Oh God, I had no idea. Roan, I'm so sorry," she said, trying to console him.

"Either party can make the choice, we've had men who choose to leave the pack as well. Leaving the pack means that they don't have to live by pack rules, but it also means being solitary and alone. My hope is, that somewhere out there, they've all found each other. Formed their own society over the years. But no one knows.

"One of the things I'd like to change is being able to petition the leader, or leaders for a separation of a relationship. That, with proper reason, you can disjoin and still remain a member of the pack. That way I could get my mother and brother back. If it's not too late."

"So that's why you agreed to the proposition?" Amelia asked, scared of his answer.

"Please understand that when my father came to me about this, I hadn't met you yet. So yes, in the beginning, it was all about righting wrongs, being able to make a difference, making things better for both groups. Amelia, I didn't know how amazing, and strong, and beautiful, and kind, and caring you were until I got to know you.

"Look at me," he pleaded as she slowly met his eyes. "I knew the instant that I met you, you were something special. You had a fire. You had spirit. You were not the woman I thought you would be, and I am *so* grateful for that."

She reached out and hugged him, just holding him. She wanted more than anything to take away the sorrow and the hurt. But she knew that's what drove him. She knew his true intentions, and they were beyond honorable. She would never dare ask to take those feelings from him.

"We'll get them back, someday," she whispered into his ear, as she felt her shoulder moisten with his tears.

They stayed like that for a while until she started to feel his emotions shifting away from sadness. They slept together that night. Just sleeping, Roan's arm thrown over her, holding her close as she enjoyed a deep and dreamless sleep.

AN AUSTRALIAN LAROUGO IN TEXAS

At some point, Amelia didn't know what time, but it was early, before their alarm, she felt Roan slip out of bed, the sounds of water running coming from the bathroom. She continued to doze, but his moving around drew her out of her sleep.

"What time is it?" she asked groggily, her eyelids still begging to close again.

"Early, go back to bed," he said in a whisper.

Amelia sat up, shaking the sleep from her mind. "No, I'm up. I'm up. The question is, why are you?"

In the darkness, she could see him shrug. "Couldn't sleep. My mind's racing. I'll sleep on the plane," he said in a clipped way. Anxiety and nerves were part of it, she could feel it.

"First time on a plane?" she guessed.

"Yes, and I may be immortal, but flying is scaring the shit out of me right now. I mean, what if we crash in the ocean?" he said, turning to her.

Now it was her turn to be nervous. She had no memory at all of the kind of shape she left her house in. But she hoped it wasn't as bad as she feared.

She watched out the window as she identified familiar landmarks. It did feel good to be home, she thought, then tried her best to push it out of her mind. This wasn't her home anymore, and she needed to start accepting that.

They were only here to tie up loose ends, delete her former life, and pack her personal belongings to be shipped back to Australia.

Roan continued to stare out the window as they drove.

"Where are all the horses?" he asked in way too serious a tone.

"I'm sorry, horses?" Amelia asked, holding back her laughter.

"Doesn't everyone in Texas have a horse or cows or something?" Amelia burst out laughing, unable to hold it in anymore.

"Now you're the one who watches too much TV," she said.

"Especially where I live, there's not a lot of horses, unless you consider the mounted patrol around the mall and Market Street," she said smiling.

"The mall?" Roan asked with curiosity.

"It's like a collection of stores, but all inside. In one really big building. We'll go a few times while we're here. I think you'll like it," she said.

"Sounds interesting," he said, as she continued to smile, thinking of all the new things she planned on showing him.

Twenty minutes later and the limo was pulling up to her one-story twenty-year-old house in an older part of the neighborhood. Her ten-year-old car still sat in the driveway, exactly where she left it.

She pulled her keys from her bag and walked to the front door using the flashlight on her phone to locate the lock. Stepping inside she turned the thermostat down. Leaving it at 75 degrees while she was away was economical, but she noticed the house had an embarrassing musty smell to it now.

She thanked the driver. And Roan was kind enough to carry their luggage, two bags at a time into the house. She turned on most of the lights, the glare forcing her eyes closed for a moment.

"That's the last of it," Roan said, letting his giant duffle bag land with a thud in the entry. "I can put my things wherever, and I'll take yours to your room," he said smiling at her.

"Actually, they all go to the same room," she said returning his smile. "Let me give you a tour."

She stepped off toward the back of the house. "This is the kitchen, where I attempt to cook. You'll notice that the refrigerator has a wide selection of frozen dinners.

"Moving on we have the living room with one couch because I couldn't afford two at the time. A fireplace, which only gets used about one month out of the year."

"Fascinating. . ."

"Through the back door, we have the smallest back yard in the neighborhood, which means it takes me all of ten minutes to mow." She flipped on the light in the

"Good morning," he said brightly, way too energetic.

"You're too cheery for me right now," she complained, throwing her pillow back over her head.

"Come on! I'm excited. Not to mention I need some coffee and breakfast."

"Sorry darling, but the kitchen's closed," she quipped from under the pillow.

Roan pulled the pillow away kissing her on the lips. "Okay, you win," she grumbled. "Breakfast and coffee, it is. But you're going to be miserable in those clothes. Just warning you," she said rolling out of bed and changing in the closet.

"Wait, first things first," Roan reminded her before they headed out the door.

"Oh, right, sorry."

She reached into his mind, turning on the desire to stay human. She was excited to take him to the mall, and even more excited to put a few miles on the card in her wallet. All the stores she'd only been able to window shop at before were now available for actual browsing and buying.

She took him first to Market Street, where they could watch the hustle and bustle of people coming in and out of the coffee shop, on their way to work. They finished their first latte, then had to wait in line for another, as Amelia's mouth began to burn.

"I have to eat. All these people are making me hungry and anxious," she said as she stood from their table outside. A man in a business suit caught her attention. He was coming from the opposite direction of the main crowd. She moved to stand in front of him, quickly influencing him that he wanted to follow her into the small outdoor restrooms. She was getting a lot quicker at it now, thankfully.

She felt much better coming back to the table. "Amelia, you've got a little . . . spot on your shirt," Roan said as she looked down. Crap, she had to wear a white shirt today too.

"Can you ask for a cup of ice?" she asked him, while she held her hand over the spot, hoping no one had noticed. He nodded, going inside the coffee shop. The ice worked well enough that you couldn't tell *exactly* what it was anymore. She put a new cute shirt on her mental shopping list.

Three lattes proved to be their limit, as they walked along the side streets, past the unopened shops. It was only 8:00, and the shops didn't open for another hour. The mall wouldn't open until 10:00. They had time to kill as Amelia's mind seemed to be in over-drive.

"Other than the heat, how do you like Texas so far?" Amelia asked.

"The heat doesn't bother me. With the proper clothes of course. It gets scorching in the Outback during the summer, so I'm used to it. But I am looking forward to this mall you keep talking about. I don't think I can say I've been to one before. At least not that I remember."

"We've got two more hours until then," she said.

"Then how about a walk. We've been walking through Perth for days, walk me through your city."

"Okay."

They walked past some of her favorite spots. She showed him some of her favorite places to eat, which she promised they would visit later in the week.

They walked all the way to the big park on the lake. Then back again to Market Street, where the expensive shops there were just opening their doors.

Walking in and out was a chore, but she decided to try something new this morning. She slathered herself with the greasy 115 SPF sunscreen she had to use at the beach when she was human.

As they walked in and out of the stores, her skin tanned much slower than it had before, making the transition so slow it was nearly unnoticeable. A trick she would definitely have to remember.

She did find a new shirt for both her and Roan at one of the boutiques. Not exactly perfect, but a fix for now, as the temperature began to rise steadily.

They walked to the mall with fifteen minutes to spare. The main doors were open, but the large anchor stores were still shuttered. They window shopped as they walked, enjoying the morning. But for some reason, Amelia was beginning to get hungry again as her anxiety also flared.

From the other end of the mall, she heard one of the wire gates being raised. They headed in that direction. "What's the rush?" Roan asked as he jogged up beside her.

"I feel like I'm starving again," she said.

"Okay, well, that should be a pretty easy fix in here," he said reaching out to grab her hand. She nodded.

As they were passing a store selling candles and other strongly scented items, a nice young woman was just opening the gate. Amelia immediately slowed and stepped up to the gate influencing her and following her into the storeroom.

The girl offered her arm to Amelia, as she was supposed to do, but once her dual teeth sunk into the woman's soft flesh, she couldn't help but drink and drink. She was drinking too much. She could tell by the heavier feeling in her stomach. It took all her resolve to pull herself free and let the girl go.

She moved quickly back to the front of the store, pulling the gate closed behind her. The girl in the storeroom would need a few minutes before she felt well enough to stand. Amelia felt the pangs of guilt replace the pangs of hunger for being so unrestrained and losing control. She didn't feel like herself right now.

"Let's go," she said to Roan as they turned and headed toward the large anchor store.

Once they were inside, they quietly ducked into a changing room together. "Hey, look at me, look at me, Amelia, you're worrying me," Roan said crouching in front of her.

"I just, I don't know what happened. I just fed a few hours ago, and all of a sudden, the hunger hit me again. I usually have longer to go between feedings," she said ashamed and worried about the girl in the fragrance shop.

"Maybe we should go home. But honestly, I'd say it's from all the excitement today," Roan suggested, as he tried to calm her down.

"You're probably right, I'll be fine. Just let me sit for a second. My anxiety has been out of control all day,"

Amelia said. She was feeling better by the minute. She stood as Roan reached for her elbow, in case she needed help.

They walked out of the dressing room to the sidelong glance of one of the store associates.

It wasn't long before they had dozens of new clothes draped over their arms, carrying them to the cashier. The woman was friendly and checked them out quickly. The total easily covered by the card that Ambrose had given her.

Going back the way they came, Amelia peeked in through the open gate of the fragrance shop, breathing a sigh of relief as she saw that the young girl was re-stocking the shelves. Fully back to normal.

Making it out of the mall and taking the long trek to Market Street, Amelia felt bad for having to call it a day. Although they had spent the entire morning out and about, she'd wanted to make a full day of it.

"I'm so sorry that today was a bust. I just need to lie down, away from all the commotion, and I'm sure I'll be 100%. Not getting enough sleep and the jet lag, and three lattes might have had an adverse reaction," she said, trying her best to brush off the day.

Back home, after the car was unloaded and she laid down on the couch, the quiet of the house seemed to help. As the roaring in her head subsided and the peacefulness of home closed in around them, she began to feel even better. Roan never left her side.

"Can I do anything?" he asked.

"No, thank you, and honestly I feel fine now. Just so many people in one place, so much commotion. It put my senses in overdrive," she said.

"You don't have to thank me, that's what I'm here for," he said smiling.

"And being back home too. There's a lot of emotions that I didn't think I'd feel. I think it's the reality that this will be the last time I'm here," Amelia said with sadness.

"Everything okay?" Roan asked as she continued to lay on the couch.

"I'm fine. Or, I'll be fine," She said sitting up. "This place was supposed to be my forever home. I had so many ideas of what my future might be. But it always included this house and this town. Now, it just seems like everything's changed."

"I'm sorry," Roan said.

"No, it's a good change. It's not that at all. I'm just a little sad to say goodbye," she said leaning in and giving him a kiss.

THE START OF SOMETHING EXCITING

The next day Amelia began the process of listing the house. She stopped in at the local Real Estate office and influenced the agent to do a walk-through and pictures all in the same day. By that afternoon the house was listed and on the market.

Considering what she paid, and what she still owed, she figured she would walk away with just over $13,000 after fees. As for the car, she decided to donate it when they left.

She hated that their one excursion to the mall had been a disaster, so she and Roan made another trip later in the week, when she was feeling more like herself. And this time she was able to tune out all the noise and the people rushing by. No more episodes so far.

They shopped and ate at some of the fancy restaurants Amelia had always wanted to try but lacked the necessary funds for. And yes, if you happened to have an extra hundred dollars or so to spare on lunch, it was worth it. According to Roan.

Walking through Market Street again, she had an idea. "When we 'join', what kind of things do you do? How do you know who's joined and who isn't?" she asked Roan.

"Well, the pack is so close we just know who's together and who isn't. How does it work here? How do you know who's with who and who isn't?" he asked.

"We wear rings on our left hand to show that we're taken." she explained as they continued to walk.

"That sounds nice," he offered.

"Would you, do you think it would be ok if we did the same?" Amelia asked shyly.

"I don't see why not. It could be our own tradition. Something new, a part of your culture and customs, and a part of mine. I think it's a great idea!" he said smiling.

"In that case . . ." Amelia said excitedly as she took a hard left, pulling him into the jewelry store just across the street from the restaurant they had eaten at earlier.

The rows of glass cases stretched out. Jewelry of all different kinds sparkled with the lighting overhead. She grabbed Roan's hand, looking through case after case until she found the section she was looking for.

A nice lady greeted them, asking when the big day was. "December, but it's an informal ceremony, so we haven't decided on an exact date," Amelia told her.

"Anything I can show you?" she asked as Amelia continued to gaze at the extensive collection in front of them. She didn't want anything too outrageous. That wasn't her style.

"What about you?" she asked Roan, who looked thoroughly out of his element.

"Let me show you something I think you would love," She said to Roan, pulling out a simple braided band with two small diamonds in the middle. "You wouldn't happen to know your size, would you?" she asked.

Roan shook his head. "Just a second," she said, excusing herself then returning will a metal loop filled with plain circles. "Size 10," she said smiling, slipping the braided band onto his left hand.

"What do you think?" he asked Amelia.

"That's entirely up to you. If you like it, then I like it."

"Can I see that one?" Roan asked pointing to a dark gray band with a single diamond set deep into the middle.

"Absolutely," she said pulling the ring for him to try.

"I love it," Amelia said. It did look like him. Dark and mysterious. If only the clerk behind the counter had any idea.

"And what about you?" he asked.

"We have a similar design for women," the clerk offered. "But my recommendation would be platinum for you. More feminine, and sophisticated." She moved behind the counter further down to the next case, pulling out a classic design.

The band was dainty with a fairly demure diamond in the center. Square with smaller ones in the band itself.

She slipped it onto Amelia's finger, who couldn't deny the immediate sense of ownership. This was the perfect ring.

"What do you think?" she asked Roan.

"I think it's perfect. But it's up to you. You're the one who has to wear it forever," he smiled, pulling her closer.

Amelia leaned into him, not caring about anyone else in the store, as she stood on her toes and kissed him.

"Can you wrap these up for us?" she asked the clerk behind the counter, handing her the credit card.

"Yes, ma'am," the clerk said as she took the rings to the back. Two beautiful blue boxes came back, along with the credit card slip. Amelia quickly signed it without looking at the price and placed the boxes in her purse.

Soon it was time for her to begin tying up the other things she'd been putting off. Her first day back at work was that coming Monday. She needed to draft her resignation letter, which she dreaded.

She debated between giving two weeks' notice and immediately resigning. She didn't have to worry about an employer review. The only thing was, she wanted to say a proper goodbye to her friends.

The other issue to consider is that from time to time, working in a doctor's office, patients came in with all kinds of injuries including cuts. And after last week's feeding binge, she didn't completely trust herself around blood. Although it hadn't happened again, she was still a little concerned and didn't want to take the chance.

Roan was probably right, her anxiety and emotions were most likely the cause. Everything Garkain and Larougo was intensified at the same time being back home and around so many people. She'd have to be more aware in large crowds, that's all.

But other than that, everything else was going well. She and Roan began to get a rhythm, and their daily routine began to take shape. The living situation was actually pretty nice. She wasn't nearly tired of his company or his good-natured teasing.

Today they were having lunch again in town. Roan had decided on one of the fancy steakhouses they'd seen. She was just finishing up her resignation letter when he politely knocked at the door to her office.

"Not to be whiner, but I'm starving. And toast for breakfast is not going to do it for me," He said, pulling her attention from the computer.

"Okay, I guess I won't let you starve. But I did warn you about my lack of cooking skills," she teased.

"And you still haven't explained how to make one of those frozen things yet, so I am at your mercy," he returned her good-natured teasing with a polite bow. "How have you been feeling lately?" he asked with genuine concern.

"Fine. I think you were right. Just have to be careful around so many people, and in certain situations. I'll try eating lunch with you, maybe that will help. I haven't had any human food since I was Unbound. Maybe a nice rare steak will do the trick," she said standing and grabbing her keys and her purse.

At the best steakhouse in town, they sat with the smells of delicious food all around them. They ordered, taking time to enjoy their meal, not feeling rushed at all. The main thing she noticed was that her food tasted bland, flavorless, all except the rare steak which oozed with juices.

"Enjoying red meat, is that a Larougo thing?" she whispered across the table to Roan.

He nodded in a half-committed way. "I'm guessing that red juice all over your plate is hitting your Garkain taste buds, but Larougo have a meat-based diet, so probably a bit of both. Is it good?"

She returned his question with a shrug. "The meat's the only thing I can taste. All the rest of it tastes like I have a cold. And the salad tastes like . . . shit," she said grinning.

"That's definitely a Larougo thing," he said returning her grin.

Dining out became an everyday thing, as Roan grew more and more comfortable, more familiar around her hometown.

Her adoptive parents never even texted or called to see if she got back to the States okay. When she did finally call to tell them she'd be moving to Australia permanently, she sensed barely a hint of emotion besides a drip of curiosity. Sadly, she expected pretty much exactly that.

Those ties were easy to break, they were so loosely tied in the first place. The girls at work were another matter. For so many years they were her best friends, her sounding boards, and her therapists. The work-family she knew and loved, would be the hardest to say goodbye to.

She had decided to resign effective immediately. As soon as she dropped the news, the girls in the office couldn't wait to get all the details about her trip, and the what and why behind her decision to move.

She remained intentionally vague, not telling them about Roan or even that much about connecting with her biological family. The story she maintained was simple and easy to remember. She visited and fell in love with the Country and the people there. She saw an opportunity to start a new life, and she took it. This version answered enough questions without allowing for much in the way of follow-up explanations.

She and Roan continued to go about the processes of selling off her things, purging herself of her former life and her former self. She removed herself from all social media, permanently deleting her accounts. It felt like, little by little, she was disappearing.

Two months after she put the house on the market, she received an acceptable offer, which she took. The remaining money in her savings account she and Roan used to tour the States, visiting all the places he put on his list.

For about a week after they returned to the States, her mother and sister called continuously, asking how things were going and when she was coming back. Telling her how they missed her. By the third week, she started letting the calls go to voicemail and answering with short quick texts instead.

There was still something off about the way they began acting toward her just after she Unbound, that she didn't quite understand. Something different and controlling. It made her feel like she was being micromanaged, under a microscope.

Roan was always supportive, always there for her. Being on their own had strengthened them in ways Amelia couldn't have predicted.

They grew closer through the months of their freedom together. Enjoying the simple things and exploring their relationship in intimate and tender ways. Amelia was happy, and she could feel that Roan was too.

After their whirlwind tour of the States, Roan spending two full days at the Smithsonian, and countless landmarks visited, it was time to return home. Her new home. Australia.

She had texted Ambrose a few times, asking about how the house in the outback was coming along. He was kind enough to send pictures, showing the progress they had already made. By the time she had booked their flight, it was still a work in progress, but it was nearly there. Huge, beautiful, and just like the picture she had sent.

Thinking more and more, Ambrose and Anatole were the ones she felt supported her most. And perhaps Roan was right. Her mother was having difficulties with the fact that Amelia achieved the life she had lost so long ago. If that were the case, she couldn't help but feel a little sorry for her.

Amelia sat looking around the empty house she worked tirelessly to afford. The home she decorated with care and took such pride in. It looked almost like the house did in the beginning, except for the paint she chose shortly after moving in.

She would miss her friends and Texas. But the house was something else altogether. Bouncing from place to place, this house was supposed to be a permanent home for her, a place to land. A home to call her own for a long time. Now, she was saying goodbye all over again, moving all her things again. But at least this time it was her choice.

"Are you sure you're ready for this?" Roan pulled her from her thoughts, as she sat on the floor of the empty living room.

The first time she left the States she carried only one suitcase. Now, as she stood in the empty living room, she stared at box after box that still needed to be loaded into the International Pod outside in the driveway.

She nodded. Sad, but excited. "I'm ready, I'm just having mixed emotions," she said as Roan patiently listened.

"Not that my life was so great, it was just familiar, predictable. From now on there's nothing predictable and nothing familiar about our future."

"I understand," Roan said hugging her close. "I love you, Amelia. I've been wanting to tell you for a while now. And I'm not just saying it because we're about to go on the craziest adventure of our long lives together. I mean it."

"I know. I love you too," she said kissing him on the lips and pulling away.

"Let's get all these boxes loaded, and we'll be ready to check-in at the hotel by the airport," she said as happily as she could, taking one last long look around, then pulling the front door closed behind her, not even bothering to look back.

They dropped her car off at the women's shelter. Donating it for a greater cause. She didn't need the money. And if she needed a car, she could buy one once they landed.

Checking in, they took their luggage down the hall to their room and got ready for bed. Living together for three months had helped to solidify them as a couple. It was nice.

She dialed her mother, letting her know that she was at the hotel by the airport and that they'd be leaving out first thing in the morning. She also let her know she'd be ditching her American phone, and she'd call from her Australian phone once they landed.

Suddenly, for no reason at all Amelia burst into tears. "I'm sorry," she said, apologizing to Roan. "I'm just really emotional right now. I don't even know why," she muttered.

"I know I made this choice, but now that it's here. Now that it's really happening. I don't know, it's like I'm on a runaway train with no way to stop it."

"Are you having second thoughts?" he asked with a touch of fear.

"Not about us, not at all. But about the responsibilities and everything we agreed to. Three months seemed like a long time to put of the inevitable. And now it's here, and I'm just overwhelmed, that's all. Tell me it's going to be okay," she pleaded with her eyes.

"It's all going to be okay. And I'll be there the whole time. No matter what. I'm here."

Roan pulled her onto the bed, curling up behind her and stroking her hair until she fell asleep.

Sometime in the night, Amelia woke up, unable to sleep. And starving. She'd been doing this for a few weeks now, starving hungry in the middle of the night for no reason. Being at home, there were few options for a midnight snack, but at the hotel . . . .

She opened the door to their room, slowly walking toward the front desk, taking her fill from the night manager in the office, then slipping back into bed as Roan continued to snore.

"I hate planes. Always have. But it was fine," he said with the same irritation.

"I have news, but I wanted to get your opinion before we began finalizing the plan," Ambrose said, motioning for his guest to sit.

Anatole walked past the drink cart, taking his time to pour a glass of gin, before sitting across from Ambrose.

He slid the phone over, Amelia's profile picture still on the screen.

"She's the right age, the right location, and the resemblance is undeniable," Anatole agreed. "What's our next move?"

"Convince my daughter to take the DNA test. Put her on the registry," Ambrose said.

"Will she be a problem?" Anatole asked, taking a sip from his glass.

"I don't think so. She'd been harboring a grudge for twenty-five years. This she'll be more than happy to do."

"Hmm, and how do we know that this Amelia will be agreeable to joining us?"

Ambrose thought for a moment before continuing. "We don't. But I have a feeling that after she learns of her heritage, of how special she is, she'll Unbind with Michelle and Robert. From the sound of her profile, she's never known a real family. Once she has been given the opportunity to rediscover her long lost past, I think she'll be more than agreeable.

"Not to mention that both Michelle and Phoebe will most likely persuade her in any way they can. A mother in search of her long-lost daughter will do anything not to lose her again. It may also take away some of her concentration on the other matter she's so dangerously pursuing.

"And Robert has made it clear that he's tired of waiting. He's asked me to bend the rules several times now, which I've continually denied. They'll convince her."

Anatole nodded, mulling. "And you're fine with the proposition we spoke of earlier?"

"I am. If Amelia truly is the child of both Phoebe and Lachlean, that means she'll be something entirely new. As long as you can persuade Roan to go along with the plan, we can convince them to create a new society."

"He's been unable to find the right mate, he'll agree. It's amazing the power family ties can have. Giving him the false hope that a new regime could bring his mother back. She's been long dead, as far as I know. But he'll be agreeable."

"Phoebe cannot succeed me. She's beginning to become unpredictable, prone to anger, possessive in a disturbing way with her children and grandchildren. And the phone calls continue. Every month or so, she checks in.

"It's my intention, once Amelia and Roan have taken their places as the new leaders of the Colony, with no council, and new laws, to cull Phoebe myself," Ambrose said, bowing his head in sadness.

"I understand," Anatole said with sympathy. "What must be done, must be done."

"Then it's decided," Ambrose said as they both stood, shaking hands.

"It's decided."